Uruguay against Brazil in the 1950 World Cup Final

ULTIMATE SOCCER

Ivor Baddiel

DK PUBLISHING, INC.

A DK PUBLISHING BOOK

Project Editor Jane Donnelly

Editor Rachel Wardley

Art Editors Sharon Grant and Ivan Finnegan

Deputy Managing Editor Dawn Sirett

US Editor Kristin Ward

Managing Art Editor

C. David Gillingwater

DTP Designers Nicola Studdart and

Cordelia Springer

Production Ruth Cobb

Picture Research Sam Ruston

Consultant Keir Radnedge

US Consultant Jim Trecker

First American Edition, 1998.
Published in the United States by DK Publishing, Inc.,
95 Madison Avenue, New York 10016

2 4 6 8 10 9 7 5 3 1

Visit us on the World Wide Web at http://www.dk.com
Copyright © 1998 Dorling Kindersley Limited, London

Main Laws of the Game pp 90-91 taken from the
1997 Laws of the Game copyright © 1997 FIFA.
Adapted with the kind permission of FIFA.

Published in Great Britain by Dorling Kindersley Limited.

Library of Congress Cataloging-in-Publication Data
Baddiel, Ivor
Soccer / by Ivor Baddiel. – 1st American ed.
p. cm.
Includes index.
ISBN 0-7894-2795-8
1. Soccer —History. 2. Soccer — Miscellanea. I. Title.
GV942.5.B33 1998
796.334 —dc21   97–36602
CIP

Color reproduction by GRB, Italy
Printed and bound in Italy by Graphicom

PASSION

ACTION

SKILLS

The Best Game in the World

Football (called soccer in the US) is the world's favorite game, and it's not hard to understand why. Football is easy to follow, it's fast and exciting, you only need a ball to play it, it can be played by any number of boys and girls, anywhere and anytime, and it brings people together from all over the world. And those are only some of its attractions!

The FIFA (Fédération Internationale de Football Association) World Cup is the ultimate highlight for every football fan and every player, so it's not surprising that the World Cup features on several pages of *Ultimate Soccer*. But football is about more than just the World Cup, and in the following pages you will be able to read about the great teams and great players, the stadiums, the cups, and the competitions that have given our game such a colorful past, and which promise so much for the future.

In all this excitement, it's important not to forget one thing in football: the game loses much of its enjoyment if we don't remember the rules of Fair Play. Playing fair makes football much more fun, and it makes winning all the more satisfying. When you turn these pages and see the stars of the past and present, you can't help realizing that the great players didn't need to foul or cheat to prove how good they were.

No matter how much of a football freak you may be, I'm sure you will find a lot in *Ultimate Soccer* that you didn't know about the game. There's always plenty to learn! That's another reason why we all think football is simply the best game in the world, and always will be.

SEPP BLATTER
General Secretary of FIFA

To All Football Fans

Football is the greatest game in the world, of that I am in no doubt. At whatever level, there is no greater feeling than being out on the pitch (field) running around, scoring a goal, making a fantastic save, playing a perfect pass, or executing a brilliantly timed tackle. But, however much we love to play, sadly the whistle blows or the park shuts and it's all over. But that's no reason to stop thinking about football or to stop building up your football knowledge. This book has enough information in it to satisfy every football fan. From how to become a professional to who scored the winning goal in the 1938 World Cup Final, it's all in here. So when the referee's whistle blows again or the park gates open, as you score that goal, make that save, play that pass, or execute that tackle, you'll not only be able to imagine that you are Pele, Banks, Platini, or Beckenbauer, you'll also know the game it happened in, the stadium it was played in, the number of people who were in the crowd, what the date was, what the final score was, and anything else that's needed to make sure that your footballing imagination is as good as your footballing feet or hands.

GIANLUCA VIALLI
Chelsea striker and Italian international

CONTENTS

Jules Rimet trophy

THE GAME

Soccer player from the 1800s

Dribbling the ball

Maracana Stadium, Rio de Janeiro

GREAT TEAMS

Match programs

Brazil after winning the 1958 World Cup

Germany's team badge

Michel Platini

GREAT PLAYERS

Ronaldo playing for Barcelona

Pele in 1970

THE FIFA WORLD CUP

Dino Zoff

1966 World Cup action

1994 FIFA World Cup mascot

1994 Brazil team

An illustration of soccer in the 1500s

THE GAME

Soccer is a massive industry. For the lucky few who participate the

rewards are great, but soccer is about more than just the players and the

coaches. It's about the fans, the stadiums, the trophies, the referees, and

many other aspects that make it a game loved by millions.

HISTORY

An illustration of a street soccer match in England in 1721

STREET VIOLENCE

The earliest record of a soccer match in Britain dates back to the 1100s. Throughout the Middle Ages, the chances of actually seeing the ball were very slim. In fact, simply watching a game would have been difficult, as it bore more resemblance to a full-scale riot than to the relatively calm spectacle of today. People were often seriously hurt and, with no stretchers to ferry them to the sidelines, they were likely to be trampled underfoot as the game continued.

This Japanese print from 1897 shows a group of Samurai warriors watching a ceremonial game of Kemari. Kemari developed from ancient Chinese football.

SOCCER, CALLED FOOTBALL in Europe and some other parts of the world, developed in England. However, no one can be certain when a round object was first kicked toward another person, as games involving a ball, teams, and some form of scoring have been around for centuries. About 3,000 years ago, the ancient Chinese played a game known as Tsu Chu (Tsu means kicking and Chu means a stuffed ball of animal skin). At about the same time in Japan they played Kemari, which involved players trying to kick a ball through two bamboo shoots. The ancient Greeks had a game called Episkyros and the Romans brought the game of Harpascum to Britain, which may have developed into soccer. By AD 217 in Britain, games involving whole villages certainly existed. These games had no rules and were often so violent that a number of kings tried to have them banned. Fortunately for the future of soccer, the games were too popular and people played on despite the bans.

An illustration from the late 1800s of an English soccer player

British private schools laid the foundations for the development of a common set of soccer rules. The Harrow School team (shown above in 1867) was among the first to play to the FA rules that were agreed upon in 1863.

RULES, WHO NEEDS RULES?

By the early 1800s in Britain, any number of different versions of soccer were being played in private schools. With no agreement on team, field, or goal sizes, and in some cases, allowing use of hands, it was impossible for schools to play each other or for the game to be played after leaving school. Thus it was that in 1848 fourteen students from Cambridge University came together to thrash out some rules. Though not universally accepted, these rules were the first attempt to give some uniformity to the game. Other rules were subsequently drawn up. The major stumbling block to achieving an agreed set of rules was whether to allow the use of hands. To decide on this, 11 representatives of clubs in London got together on October 26, 1863 to form the Football Association (FA). By December 8 of that year they had agreed on a set of rules.

Soccer fans have always been noisy and enthusiastic. In the early days, they used rattles.

Charles Alcock, one of the early secretaries of the English FA

Left, illustrations from the late 1800s showing how to chest the ball and how not to head the ball. Note the large size of the ball compared to the modern version.

SOCCER'S FIRST CUP COMPETITION

As soccer continued to grow in Britain, it wasn't long before a knockout cup competition was suggested. In 1871, the then secretary of the English FA, Charles Alcock, proposed a tournament based on one that had been played at Harrow School. The following year the world's oldest soccer cup competition, the English FA Cup, was born. The competition was completed in just 13 matches. Wanderers upset the betting sheets by beating the favored Royal Engineers 1-0 in the Final, which was watched by 2,000 spectators.

From the very beginning, important FA Cup matches attracted huge crowds and they continue to do so today.

THE ENGLISH LEAGUE

In 1885 the English FA legalized professionalism, allowing clubs to pay players. This meant that more games needed to be played to pay players' salaries. William McGregor of Aston Villa proposed the idea of home and away games. It was adopted by 12 clubs and on March 22, 1888 the English Football League was formed.

William McGregor, founder of the English Football League

One of the early English League medals won by Aston Villa in 1897

When English players became professionals their salaries were paid out of match ticket sales. FA Cup matches also helped to support players' salaries. The FA Cup Final in 1901 (above) drew a record crowd of 114,815 to see Tottenham Hotspur play Sheffield United. The match was drawn, but Tottenham won the replay.

As the game grew in popularity, a wide range of books and souvenirs was produced to satisfy the fans' demands.

A GREAT EXPORT

Britain was responsible for the introduction of soccer to many other parts of the world. The first place to be infected was Argentina when, in 1865, British residents founded the Buenos Aires Football Club. In 1879 the English Football Club was set up in Denmark, and in Switzerland students who had learned the game from their British counterparts set up St. Gallen Football Club. In 1888, British businessmen set up a club in Germany. The worldwide spread of the game had begun.

FIFA IS FORMED

By 1903 there was talk of creating an international soccer federation, and in 1904 the Federation Internationale de Football Association, or FIFA, was formed. Soccer continued to grow worldwide, most notably in Europe and South America, and by 1939 membership of FIFA had grown to more than 50 countries.

Today membership of FIFA stands at almost 200 nations, making soccer the world's greatest ball game.

Soccer was first played in Denmark in the late 1800s. The first Copenhagen team for the 1886-87 season is shown above.

FROM SIMPLE BEGINNINGS

Soccer has come a long way in the last 150 years. Television coverage and sponsorship have turned it into a multibillion dollar global industry. The top players are now media stars worth millions and they have dedicated physical therapists and trainers to help them maintain optimum levels of fitness.

Soccer training consisted of a brisk walk for the 1906 West Bromwich Albion team. The training facilities available to players have changed a great deal since then.

THEN AND NOW

I F YOU WERE TO TRAVEL back in time and stumble upon a soccer match in the 1890s, things would not be that unfamiliar. The essence of the game has remained the same. However, since that time, soccer has seen some changes. It is now the world's most popular sport and has spawned a huge range of merchandise and memorabilia. Over the decades, changing fashions and new materials have transformed the basic uniform and soccer shoes, and huge sums of money have been invested to produce the most performance-enhancing balls and shoes.

MERCHANDISE
At one time, the only place you would see pictures of soccer players, other than in newspapers, was on cards in cigarette packages. Today, it's possible to buy almost anything, from bedsheets to clocks and bottles of wine, displaying the latest stars.

In the early 1900s soccer shoes were made of heavy leather.

PROGRAMS

Over the years, programs have become glossy color magazines, crammed with action pictures, facts, and figures.

The earliest programs were very basic, consisting of just one sheet of paper. Today they are more like magazines, but the early ones are considerably more valuable.

Match cards, such as this one from 1875, were the forerunners of today's magazine-style programs.

Today, soccer shoes are designed to give comfort and maximum performance.

SHOES
In the 1800s before soccer shoes were widely available, some players nailed studs into their ordinary working boots. Today's shoes are sleek and colorful compared to the early, heavy-leather ankle-high boots.

TICKET PRICES
A ticket for the first official international match between England and Scotland in 1872 cost one shilling (five pence). The cheapest tickets for an England match during the 1996 European Championship cost £15 ($9.00). The most expensive were £130 ($80.00).

This illustration from the 1600s shows the bladder of a "pallone," an early Italian soccer ball, being inflated.

Below, a modern-day soccer ball used in the 1996 European Championship.

SOCCER BALLS

The first soccer balls were animal bladders encased in leather. They were laced together by hand and often lost their shape during a game. They were also prone to water retention, making them increase in weight considerably if it rained. Modern soccer balls use a number of different materials and have a plastic coating, which avoids the problem of water retention. They are lighter and tend to keep their shape well.

The pre-1940s soccer ball (above) wasn't waterproof and the final seam had to be laced up.

In the early 1900s, shorts and shirts were long.

In the 1950s, shirts resembled rugby shirts.

By the 1970s, shorts were shorter and shirts slim-fitting.

Short lengths continue to vary from one decade to the next. These are from the 1980s.

Today, shorts are mid-length. Shirts are loose-fitting.

SHIRTS

Soccer shirts have changed a great deal over the years. At one time they were made of cotton, had lace-up collars, and no writing on them. Nowadays they are made of synthetic material, which in some cases has been specifically designed to give maximum ventilation. They will almost inevitably bear a sponsor's name on the front.

SHORTS

The main change to shorts has been their length. At one time, they were knee-length, but today's soccer players wear them somewhat shorter.

Modern goalkeepers' gloves have lots of padding.

GLOVES

Originally, goalkeepers wore simple, cotton gloves. Today's gloves have heavy padding, textured surfaces, and adhesive strips to keep them on.

SOCCER GAMES

Air soccer and table soccer were the first games to try to re-create real soccer in people's living rooms. Although they are still very enjoyable, today's advanced technology means that the computer screen, rather than the floor or table, now dominates soccer's indoor playing arena.

Early goalkeepers wore plain shirts and shorts.

Modern goalkeepers wear colorful uniforms.

GOALKEEPERS' UNIFORM

Until recently, goalkeepers' shirts were green, yellow, or white. They have undergone great changes and are now multicolored and padded.

RULES AND RULE CHANGES

THE BASIC GOAL OF SOCCER has remained the same, but it is a developing game. At one time no substitutes were allowed; a referee could award a goal if a player used his hands to stop a ball from crossing the goal line; and the goalkeeper could pick up the ball from a back pass. Since 1913, recognized international rules have been in operation, but over the years there have been many changes. Some have had a profound effect on the game, while others have just tweaked it a little. In general, the intention is to create an exciting spectacle in which those officiating can do their jobs with clarity and consistency.

Referees and assistant referees have the difficult task of balancing rules with allowing exciting, flowing soccer.

SOME CHANGES FOR THE BETTER

1913: Opposing players to go back 10 yards (9.2 meters) when a free kick is being taken.
1924: Away uniform design to be worn by the visiting team if uniform colors are the same.
1925: Players to have two feet on the ground when taking a throw-in.
1937: Arc of circle drawn outside the penalty area.
1951: Obstruction included as an offense punishable by an indirect free kick.
1976: Red and yellow cards introduced.
1981: Three points for a win introduced.
1989: A player level with the last outfield defender is no longer offside.
1992: Pass back rule introduced. The goalkeeper is not allowed to pick the ball up if it is kicked back by one of his or her own players.

A referee cautioning a player with a yellow card.

A corner kick is taken from the corner arc next to the flag.

THE SIMPLEST GAME RULES OF 1862 (ADOPTED BY FIFA IN 1863)

1. A goal is scored whenever the ball is forced through the goal and under the bar, except be it thrown by hand.

2. Hands may be used only to stop the ball and place it on the ground before the feet.

3. Kicks must be aimed only at the ball.

4. A player may not kick at the ball while it is in the air.

5. No tripping up or heel kicking is allowed.

6. Whenever the ball is kicked beyond the side flags, it must be returned by the player who kicked it, from the spot where it passed the flag line, in a straight line toward the middle of the ground.

7. When a ball is kicked behind the line of the goal, it shall be kicked off from that line by one of the team whose goal it is.

8. No opposite player may stand within six paces of the kicker when he is kicking off.

9. A player is out of play (offside) immediately he is in front of the ball, and he must return behind the ball as soon as possible. If the ball be kicked by his own team past a player, he may not touch it, kick it, nor advance until one of the other team has first kicked it or one of his own team having followed it up, has been able, when in front of him, to kick it.

10. No charging is allowed when a player is out of play, i.e., immediately the ball is behind him.

THE FUTURE

The game continues to evolve. It is unlikely that the use of hands is ever going to be permitted, but who knows what lies ahead? Here are some possible changes.

Video Referees: Video could have a major part to play in the future of soccer refereeing.
Sin Bin: A third card may be introduced, allowing the referee to order a player to leave the field for ten minutes.
Offside: A heated issue; some advocate abolishing the offside rule altogether.

Since 1913, opposing players have been made to stand 10 yards (9.2 meters) from where a free kick is taken.

Another future change could see the current throw-in replaced with a kick-in.

TECHNIQUES AND TACTICS

WHATEVER POSITION YOU play, there are many techniques that need to be mastered. Positional play if you're a goalkeeper, the timing of a tackle if you're a defender, accurate passing if you're a midfielder, and beating your marker if you're an attacker are just some of the many different skills players need to work on. Here are some of the key techniques to learn.

Goalkeepers need to anticipate where the ball is going and move quickly into position to stop the shot.

Zoff, playing for Italy, shouts instructions to the rest of his defense.

COMMANDING THE GOAL AREA
A goalkeeper must command his or her defense confidently. It is vital that defenders know when to leave the ball for the keeper, when to pass it back, or when to kick it out of play. Any shout must be clear and loud.

Goalkeeping

The best goalkeepers are extremely agile and have razor-sharp reflexes. As a goalkeeper your main priority is to stop the ball from going into the net. When making a save, any part of your body can be utilized, but your main assets will always be your hands.

When catching a high ball, form your hands into a "w" shape with your fingers spread out and your thumbs almost touching. Your forearms should be slightly bent to take the power out of the shot.

STOPPING THE BALL
A goalkeeper should always try leaping up to catch high shots. If you cannot catch a high ball, it is best to punch it out, using both fists clenched tightly together. For chest-high shots, place yourself in line with the ball and cushion the shot with your body, cupping your hands around the ball. For shots out of your immediate reach, you may have to dive and palm the ball away, angling your hands to divert the ball around the post or over the bar.

Schmeichel closes the angle to try to block Vialli's goal in a match between Manchester United and Chelsea.

POSITIONAL PLAY
As a goalkeeper it is crucial to concentrate at all times, positioning yourself so that you are always between the ball and the goal. If an attacker is heading straight toward the goal, it is important to "narrow the angle." This means gradually moving toward the ball, giving the attacker less of the goal to aim at.

Defending

As a defender it is your job to stop opposing attackers from gaining possession of the ball, and to start to build an attack for your own team. It is a role that demands coordination, as well as strength and determination.

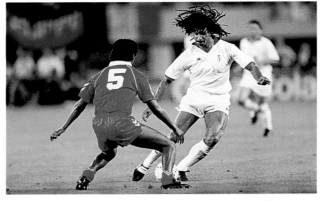

Aldair of Portuguese club Benfica closely marking Ruud Gullit of AC Milan in the European Cup Final in 1990.

Always watch the ball when tackling.

BLOCK TACKLE
There are two main tackles, a block tackle and a sliding tackle. To block tackle, strike the ball just as your opponent is about to pass it. Using all your weight, put the inside of your foot as close to the center of the ball as possible. You need to remain on your feet so you can gain possession of the ball after winning the tackle.

Croatia's Vlaovic, the victim of a sliding tackle by Portugal's Sousa

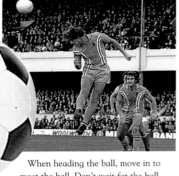

When heading the ball, move in to meet the ball. Don't wait for the ball to come to you.

MARKING
Marking involves staying close to an opponent to stop them from passing, shooting, or receiving the ball. When marking another player, it is important to remain between that player and the goal, or "goalside" as it is known. The attacker will try to get away from you, so you must concentrate not just on where the ball is, but also on where the attacker is going.

A good marker will deny an opponent the space he needs to use the ball well.

DEFENSIVE HEADING
A defensive header is meant to clear the ball as far away as possible. The timing of your run and jump is very important in order to get as much power into the header as possible and the more height you can get into your jump, the better. Remember to use your forehead, to head the ball upward, and to always hit the bottom half of the ball.

SLIDING TACKLE
A successful sliding tackle requires expert timing. It is used to clear the ball rather than gain possession. When your opponent has the ball, run toward them and slide into the tackle. Bend your supporting leg while stretching out the other one.

Try to time your jump so that you head the ball when you are at your highest point.

Midfield

Great midfield players are often known as "generals" because of the way their influence extends to every part of the game. Midfielders may be required to help the defense or the offense. They have the freedom to roam in and out of defense or offense whenever needed.

Lothar Matthäus for Germany hitting a long pass

BALL CONTROL

Mastery of the ball is crucial. Bringing the ball under control in one movement can give midfield players those extra few seconds, allowing them to pass the ball with pinpoint accuracy.

To control a high ball, cushion it on your chest.

TRAPPING

One of the main ways to control the ball is trapping. This involves stopping the ball dead between the sole of your foot and the ground. As the ball comes toward you, lift up your foot and let the ball wedge itself under your shoe. Keeping your eye on the ball, and timing are both very important.

Trapping the ball is aided by the studs on the sole of your shoe.

LONG PASSES

Knowing when to play a short ball to a nearby colleague or hit a long pass upfield is all part of the midfielder's art. A long or lofted pass can be played by giving yourself a short run up to the ball and approaching it at an angle. To get the height you need, lean back slightly as you are about to strike the ball and hit it at the bottom with your instep.

SHORT PASSES

Turn your leg outward from the hip and use the inside of your foot to push pass.

To hit a short push pass accurately to another player, use the inside part of your foot. Keep the other foot nearby and your eye on the ball. Strike the middle of the ball, keeping it low. The ball will travel in the direction you are facing. Ideally, it should be played just in front of your teammate.

Practice your dribbling by setting up a row of cones.

Don't kick the ball too far ahead.

Keep the ball close to your foot.

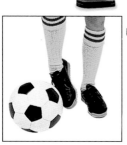
Use the outside of your foot to straighten the ball.

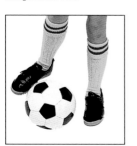
Push the ball forward a little with the inside of your foot.

DRIBBLING

Watching midfield players run with the ball past opponents is one of the most exciting aspects of soccer, but it involves a high level of skill. When dribbling, it is important to keep control of the ball so that you can change direction at any time. The ball should be kept in front of you by using gentle taps from either the inside or outside of your foot. If you are confronted by an opponent, push the ball one way and when the player moves in that direction, take the ball the other way to go past him or her.

Skillful dribbling confuses opponents and makes it hard for them to tackle you.

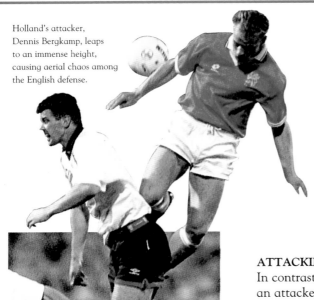

Holland's attacker, Dennis Bergkamp, leaps to an immense height, causing aerial chaos among the English defense.

Attacking

In addition to being an accurate header and striker of the ball, to be a good goalscorer, an attacker has to learn how to be in the right place at the right time. He or she has to anticipate passes and crosses, and run into position at the right time to avoid opponents.

Diego Maradona loses his Italian opponent, defender Franco Baresi.

ATTACKING HEADERS

In contrast to a defensive header, as an attacker attempting to head the ball into the goal you should firmly head the ball down. This means that you need to get a great deal of spring into your jump so you not only outleap the defenders, but also get over the ball. Aim your header to bounce close to the goal line so that it is more difficult for the keeper to reach. As with a defensive header, the forehead should be used and it is important to attack the ball with confidence and not just dive in hopefully.

LOSING YOUR MARKER

A great striker will manage to make space for him or herself no matter how tightly he or she is being marked. To do this, it is important to change direction or stop suddenly when making a run in order to confuse the defender. Once you have broken free from your marker, the ball should be played to you quickly before the defender has a chance to catch you. It is important to remember that on average a player has the ball for only three minutes in a game, so a lot of the work has to be done away from the ball.

When shooting, don't lean back too far or the ball will go over the bar. To keep the ball low, you must lean over it and kick the top half.

Spread out your arms to help you balance.

Keep your eye on the ball and your opponent as he or she moves in to tackle.

Push the ball one way and when the defender moves in that direction, push the ball away from him or her.

SHOOTING

Whether it is a tap-in, a drive from outside the penalty area, or a volley that almost bursts through the net, if you don't shoot you won't score. A good shot should combine power and accuracy. To do this with the ball on the ground, place your supporting foot close to the ball and using the inside of your shooting foot, take a small backswing and strike the ball cleanly in the middle.

FORMATIONS

WITHIN THE RULES as they stand, a team can adopt whatever formation it likes. If they wished, teams could play with a goalkeeper and ten attackers all charging after the ball. Indeed, the first soccer games were probably played very much in that way. However, since then the game has developed and over the years various formations have been employed in order to find that elusive winning formula. Here are some of the most important.

The most effective teams adopt a formation (an arrangement of players) that gives them the best "shape" to carry out the tactics developed by the coach or manager.

The Preston North End team that won the English League and FA Cup in 1889

CLASSIC FORMATION

This formation, with two fullbacks, a right-, center-, and left-halfback, and five forwards (2-3-5), although very attack-minded, was the first real attempt to play a more defensive system. It was used by England and Scotland in the mid-1880s and, most successfully, by Preston North End when they became the first English team to win the English League and FA Cup "double" in 1889.

The 1927 English FA Cup winners, Arsenal, that used the WM formation

WM FORMATION

In 1925, changes to the offside law gave rise to a massive increase in the number of goals scored. To combat this, English soccer player Charlie Buchan of Arsenal and his manager Herbert Chapman developed the WM formation. In this system the center halfback was brought back into defense to mark the opposing center forward, and both inside forwards were played just behind the attack in order to create goalscoring chances. Arsenal used this formation very successfully in the 1930s and it became extremely popular the world over.

Charlie Buchan and the Arsenal team. Buchan developed the WM formation with his manager.

Herbert Chapman

Forwards

Halfbacks

Fullbacks

Attackers span the width of the field

CLASSIC 2-3-5 FORMATION

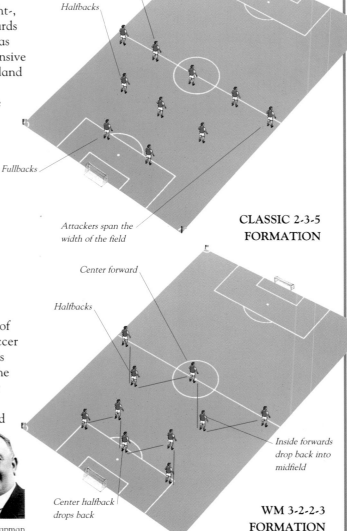

Center forward

Halfbacks

Inside forwards drop back into midfield

Center halfback drops back

WM 3-2-2-3 FORMATION

4-2-4 FORMATION AND VARIATIONS

Devised by the great Hungarian team of the early 1950s, the 4-2-4 formation was used to great effect by the 1958 Brazilian World Cup winning team. It was another very attack-minded system. The two fullbacks were expected to push forward, effectively creating a 2-4-4 set-up at times. Later Brazilian teams pulled one of the wingers back into midfield, giving a 4-3-3 formation. The England World Cup winning team of 1966 played a 4-4-2 system, which was more defensive. The fullbacks were not expected to push forward, and one of the midfielders played just in front of the back four to act as a defensive screen.

Hungary using the 4-2-4 formation against England in 1953

England playing the 4-4-2 system against Portugal in their 1966 World Cup semifinal

Fullbacks pushed forward along the wings

Winger moved back into midfield

Midfielders link attack and defense.

Defense consists of two fullbacks and two center backs.

4-2-4 FORMATION AND 4-3-3 FORMATION

SWEEPER SYSTEM

A sweeper is a defender who moves freely behind the defense. Playing a sweeper behind the back four was originally part of the very defensive "catenaccio" system developed in Italy. The sweeper would roam around behind the defense attempting to catch any attackers who might break through. This system, which was used very effectively by Italian club teams, made it extremely hard for opposing sides to score goals.

However, Franz Beckenbauer turned the sweeper's role into a far more attacking one by sometimes playing in front of the back four and, occasionally, bringing the ball forward himself, well into the opponents' half.

One of the great sweepers, Franz Beckenbauer

Only two forwards

Three midfielders

Back four

Sweeper is the last line of defense

SWEEPER SYSTEM

FORMATIONS TODAY

The 5-3-2 system and the 4-4-2 system are currently vying for predominance. A number of teams are favoring a return to the 4-4-2 system. In reality, the 5-3-2 formation is a system that fluctuates, effectively making a 3-5-2 formation in attacking situations and a 5-3-2 formation in defense.

Every new attacking formation quickly breeds a new defensive system for defeating it. Consequently, it is generally easier to produce effective defensive formations than successful attacking ones.

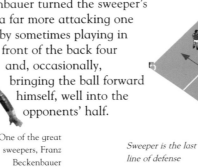

Italy's Paolo Maldini is one of the most renowned attacking fullbacks.

Back four

This midfielder plays in front of the defense.

Attacking fullbacks

This midfielder plays behind the attack.

Three central defenders

5-3-2 AND 4-4-2 FORMATIONS

CHAMPIONSHIPS AND TROPHIES

WINNING THE WORLD CUP is the pinnacle of any player's career, but it would take an awfully long time to fill a trophy cabinet if there was nothing else to play for. Thankfully, throughout the world there are many other championships at both international and club level. Each one is eagerly sought after, for as any player who has ever battled through numerous qualifying matches will confirm, there is no feeling in the world like raising a trophy in front of thousands of jubilant supporters.

National Team Competitions

Jules Rimet trophy

Jürgen Klinsmann and his teammates celebrating Germany's victory over the Czech Republic in the 1996 European Championship Final

EUROPEAN CHAMPIONSHIP
The brainchild of Frenchman Henri Delaunay, the European Championship finals have been held every four years since 1960. Over the years, the format has changed and currently it resembles a World Cup for Europe, with teams taking part in a two-year qualifying tournament to earn the right to compete in the final rounds. Only the hosts gain automatic entry to the final rounds.

Henri Delaunay European Championship trophy

WORLD CUP FOR WOMEN
The women's World Cup was first held in 1991. Just like the men's World Cup, teams take part in a qualifying tournament to enter the final rounds, which are hosted by one nation. Holders and hosts gain automatic entry to the final rounds.

The Norway women's team, celebrating their World Cup victory in 1995

The original men's World Cup trophy was named after Jules Rimet. Brazil was allowed to keep this trophy after winning the World Cup for a third time in 1970. It was later stolen and melted down for its gold content. The current World Cup trophy was first presented in 1974.

COPA AMERICA (ORIGINALLY CALLED SOUTH AMERICAN CHAMPIONSHIP)

Originally open to the ten members of South America's governing body of soccer, CONMEBOL, this is the longest running international tournament. First held in 1910, the tournament has been through a number of changes. Since 1993, Mexico and the US have taken part and the format consists of three groups of four, from which eight proceed to a knockout phase.

Copa America

Sergio Martinez of Uruguay raises the Copa America in 1995.

CENTRAL AMERICAN CHAMPIONSHIP

This championship began in 1941 and is held every two years.

ASIAN CUP AND OCEANIA CUP

The Asian Cup has been running since 1956, and is competed for every four years. The Oceania Cup competition has been held in 1973 and 1980.

Asian Cup

Asian Cup finalists for the fourth time in a row, Saudi Arabia celebrate their victory in 1996.

European Cup

South African goalscorer Mark Williams with the African Nations Cup in 1996

AFRICAN NATIONS CUP

Only Egypt, Ethiopia, and Sudan took part in the first finals of this tournament in 1957, but it has since grown to become a continent-wide competition. Since 1992, 12 teams have competed in the final rounds. The hosts and holders automatically qualify for the finals tournament.

African Nations Cup

Nigeria's victorious men's team with their Olympic gold medals in 1996

OLYMPICS

Soccer has been an Olympic sport for men since 1908. It has been through a number of changes, mainly due to the original problems of trying to keep it open only to amateurs. The current tournament, for which a worldwide, qualifying tournament is played, is for national, professional Under-23 teams. The 1996 Games saw the first women's soccer tournament to be played at an Olympics.

Club Competitions

Italian team Juventus celebrates its World Club Championship victory in Tokyo in 1996.

World Club Cup

WORLD CLUB CHAMPIONSHIP

The World Club Championship has been played between the winners of the European Cup and the South American Copa Libertadores since 1960. Originally a two-leg home and away tie was used, but since 1980 a single match, known as the Toyota Cup, has been played in Tokyo to decide the Championship.

AFRICAN CLUB COMPETITIONS

There are three main African club competitions. The African Cup of Champion Clubs is open to the League champions of each country and the African Cup Winners' Cup is for the knockout Cup winners from each country. A more recent addition is the CAF Cup for League runners-up.

African Cup of Champion Clubs

Juventus celebrate winning the Italian Serie A in 1996 which enabled them to qualify for the European Cup.

Players from Argentinian team River Plate celebrate their Copa Libertadores victory in 1996.

EUROPEAN CLUB COMPETITIONS

There are three annual club competitions in Europe. The most prestigious is the European Cup (officially European Champions League), which until recently was competed for by the League champions of each country. It has now been extended to include the League runners-up of the stronger nations. European teams who win their country's knockout Cup competition enter the European Cup Winners' Cup. The UEFA Cup, formerly known as the Fairs Cup, is usually competed for by the top clubs of a country who have not qualified for either of the other two European club events.

COPA LIBERTADORES

The Copa Libertadores is South America's main club competition. Played annually since 1960, it is the equivalent of the European Cup and is competed for by the League champions of each South American country.

Copa Libertadores

STADIUMS

AS LONG AS YOU have a ball, a couple of tin cans for goalposts, and some space, it's possible to play soccer just about anywhere. However, there are some places where the atmosphere makes the game that little bit special. Some stadiums are almost as famous as the players and clubs that have played there.

MARACANA, RIO DE JANEIRO, BRAZIL

The Maracana, which takes its name from a minor river that runs nearby, is the largest stadium in the world. Its current capacity is 120,000. A world record of 199,854 people turned up at the Maracana to see Brazil face Uruguay in the 1950 World Cup Final. Brazil needed only a tie to become champions, but the majority of the crowd left disappointed as Uruguay won 2-1. The Maracana also holds the attendance record for a club match. This was achieved in 1963 when 177,656 spectators watched a match between Brazilian clubs Flamengo and Fluminense.

The Maracana Stadium opened in 1950, but was not completed until 1965.

HAMPDEN PARK, GLASGOW, SCOTLAND

Until the Maracana opened, Hampden Park was the largest stadium in the world. In 1937, 149,415 people (a European record) saw Scotland defeat England 3-1, and just seven days later 147,365 spectators crammed in for the Scottish Cup Final between Celtic and Aberdeen. By the mid-1970s, the stadium was in need of repair, and work to convert it into a 50,000-seat venue began.

The Azteca Stadium in Mexico during the opening ceremony of the 1986 World Cup

ESTADIO GUILLERMO CAÑEDO, MEXICO CITY, MEXICO

Formerly known as the Azteca, this is the only stadium to have played host to two World Cup Finals, in 1970 and 1986. It was built for the 1968 Olympics, but the first game played there was in 1966, when Mexico took on Italian club Torino. The stadium has a capacity of 110,000, and a lower tier only 33 feet (10 meters) from the field. It was renamed Estadio Guillermo Cañedo in 1997.

BERNABEU, MADRID, SPAIN

After the Nuevo Chamartin Stadium was ravaged in Spain's civil war, Real Madrid's president, Santiago Bernabeu, raised 41 million pesetas to build a new

The Bernabeu Stadium, the home of Real Madrid

one. The 105,000-capacity Bernabeu Stadium stands proudly on Madrid's most prestigious street, Castellana. It opened in 1947 and was made famous by Real Madrid's domination of the European Cup in the 1950s. It has hosted three European Cup Finals, in addition to the 1982 World Cup Final between Italy and West Germany.

The Nou Camp Stadium, home to the Barcelona team

NOU CAMP, BARCELONA, SPAIN

Completed in 1957 at a cost of 66 million pesetas, the Nou Camp Stadium has a capacity of 115,000, just big enough to house the 110,000 members who make Barcelona the world's biggest club. However, with work constantly going on, as the club's membership increases, so should capacity. In 1971, an indoor sports hall was opened. There is also a 16,500-capacity mini-stadium across a walkway where Barcelona's reserve team plays in the Spanish lower divisions.

Inside the amazing San Siro Stadium during the 1990 World Cup finals tournament

SAN SIRO, MILAN, ITALY

Home to Italian clubs AC Milan and Internazionale, the San Siro, or Giuseppe Meazza Stadium, is one of the great wonders of the modern soccer-playing world. From an original capacity of 35,000 in 1926, it has grown considerably. In 1990, eleven cylindrical towers allowed for a third tier and a roof and increased the capacity to 83,000 in time for the World Cup finals tournament. However, this created a problem for the groundskeepers since the roof prevents light and rain from reaching the field.

WEMBLEY STADIUM, LONDON, ENGLAND

With its twin towers, Wembley Stadium is without a doubt the most famous soccer arena in the world. The legendary Pele called it the church of soccer and said, "Wembley is the home of the beautiful game." Originally built to be the centerpiece of the British Empire Exhibition in 1924, the stadium was actually completed in 1923 and had a capacity of 127,000. That year it staged the historic FA Cup Final between West Ham and Bolton Wanderers. More than 200,000 people turned up and had to be dispersed by police before the game could begin. As England's national stadium, it now stages all of the English FA Cup Finals.

Today, Wembley is an all-seater stadium with a capacity of 80,000. It will soon be undergoing a major face-lift, but the twin towers are two features that won't be disappearing.

THE DEVELOPING GAME

AT ONE TIME NO WORLD CUP finals tournament was complete without one of the major national teams inflicting a devastating defeat upon one of the weaker national teams. However, there are no easy games anymore. All over the world interest in soccer is growing among women and men, and many national teams are developing rapidly. The future of the game is surely guaranteed.

The number of women involved in both officiating and playing the game is growing.

TALENTED US PLAYERS
Talented soccer players in the US are often good all-around athletes who are soon signed up by major baseball, basketball, and football teams. So although soccer has thrived at college level, until the advent of Major League Soccer in 1996, top players rarely reached professional level.

Lalas (above right) is one of the best-known US players.

UNITED STATES OF AMERICA
Many people might think that the US has only recently taken up soccer, but in fact they have been competing for more than 100 years. The US also made a great success of hosting the 1994 World Cup finals. They performed extremely well, too, losing only 1-0 to Brazil in the second round. In 1995, they reached the semifinals of the Copa America, beating Argentina 3-0 on the way.

The US men's team celebrates a victory against England in 1994 in a friendly match. John Harkes holds the trophy.

The opening ceremony of the 1996 Olympic Games in the US. The attendance figures for the Olympic soccer tournament were much higher than anticipated, indicating the increasing popularity of the game in the US.

NEW US LEAGUE
In 1996, a new outdoor professional league, called Major League Soccer, filled the gap left by the collapse of the North American Soccer League (NASL). In addition to overseas stars, the new league has encouraged more homegrown players to become involved. Attendance figures have been good.

Women's soccer is rapidly gaining recognition. Norway (left) is one of the strongest international teams, shown here in their victorious match against the US in the women's 1995 World Cup semifinals.

Nigeria celebrates its 3-2 victory over Argentina in the 1996 Olympic Final for Under-23 national teams.

THE WOMEN'S GAME

FIFA's comment that the future of soccer is feminine is an indication of the rapid growth of the women's game. FIFA now has a women's committee and even though there are currently no professional leagues, Italy, Japan, and the US have semi-professional leagues, and many women players are paid. The women's World Cup was first held in China in 1991, and women's soccer became an Olympic sport for the first time at Atlanta in 1996. Women's soccer is also currently the fastest-growing sport in Britain and the most popular women's sport in the US with around eight million participants.

China at the women's Olympic tournament in 1996

Guido Buchwald and Thomas Berthold for Germany and Sun Hong Hwang for South Korea during the 1994 World Cup finals tournament. South Korea scored two goals against Germany, although they eventually lost 2-3.

AFRICA

Pele predicted that an African nation would win the World Cup by the year 2000. When Cameroon defeated holders Argentina in the opening game of the 1990 World Cup finals tournament, people began to understand why. Since then African national teams, in particular Nigeria, have continued to impress with their flowing, attacking soccer. Their success is reflected in African teams being awarded five places at the 1998 World Cup finals tournament, compared with only three places in 1994. At club level the African game suffers from poor administration and facilities, and all the continent's best players join European clubs.

The famous opening match in the 1990 World Cup finals tournament when Cameroon won 1-0 against Argentina with a goal by Oman Biyik

ASIA

Half of the world's registered soccer players are from Asia. Unfortunately, the huge size of the continent makes organizing international competitions difficult. However, with growing economic prosperity in some parts of the region, more money has come into the game in recent years. This has led to growth in the number of professional leagues and more interest from TV companies. Japan's big money J-League has also attracted a number of top foreign players and coaches. Finally, with FIFA awarding the 2002 World Cup to Japan and South Korea jointly, Asian interest in soccer is bound to rise even more in forthcoming years.

Peng Weiguo for China, and Hirochi Nanami and Kazuyoshi Miura for Japan in the 1996 Asian Cup

A British youth team, Rucknolt, in 1907

SO YOU WANT TO BECOME A PROFESSIONAL

THERE CAN BE LITTLE DOUBT that being a top professional soccer player today has many rewards, not least of which is that you can spend most of your time actually playing the game you love. But those who dream of one day scoring the winning goal in a World Cup Final should be warned. Only very, very few players make it to the top and they have to work extremely hard to get there.

Whether you like to play offense or defense, there will be specialized techniques to practice and master.

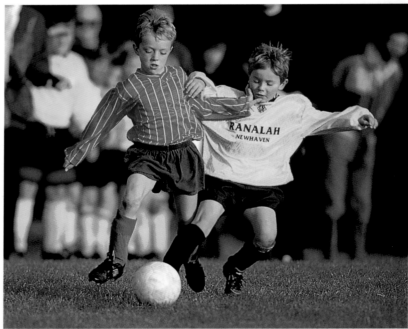

The basic skills of soccer can be picked up at a very early age.

STEP 1: JOIN UP

Daydreaming about soccer isn't enough! You have to get out onto the field and play the game. The first thing to do is to join a team. It's a good idea to join one affiliated with the US Soccer Federation so that you can take part in official competitions, but you should also play with your elementary, junior, or high school teams to develop your soccer skills.

Junior players in China prepare for soccer trials.

STEP 2: BEING SPOTTED

Obviously the next step, that of becoming a good player, depends on a mixture of natural talent and practice. Promising players are likely to be spotted by one of the many scouts the US Soccer Federation annually sends around the country. The scouts attend all the youth competitions to identify the top prospects, who are then monitored and perhaps invited to an Under-14 (age-group) training camp at the Olympic training center in California. At this age, the process of "becoming a pro" really starts. Players are taught individual as well as team-oriented skills and begin to experience a higher intensity atmosphere and training rigors while still being able to simply enjoy the game.

Breaking for lunch at a soccer training school

Starting young with Holland's Ajax Under-12 team

STEP 3: TALENT SCOUTS

With the advent of Major League Soccer in the US, those 12 teams will be scouting colleges heavily in search of talent. This will provide a very good outlet for young hopefuls.

Club scouts looking for gifted young players may attend local matches.

STEP 4: MAKING CONTACTS

While participating in Federation- or school-sanctioned events, you should also familiarize yourself with the soccer officials in your state. Your coach can usually help with this process. Visit with local coaches and invite them to watch you play. Keep playing at the college level. If college is not part of your plans, inquire about joining Project 40, a Federation/Major League Soccer initiative.

It takes years of experience to score that goal.

Players at the Ajax training school in Holland

STEP 5: MAKING THE DREAM COME TRUE

However you pursue your dream of becoming a professional soccer player, remember the most important thing is to practice and play as much as possible.

WHAT DOES EVERYONE DO?

THE STARS OF ANY soccer match are the players. However, there are many other people involved who ensure that those players are fit and healthy, understand what tactics they are supposed to be playing, don't trip over divots on the field, and, of course, get paid. Remember, soccer is international and roles and titles vary depending on where the game is being played.

Marcello Lippi, the Juventus Manager, in 1996

THE COACH

In the US, soccer teams are mainly directed by someone called a coach. The coach sets the strategy, calls the shots, and makes the philosophical decisions, as well as handling the team's day-to-day training and preparation (with a team of assistants). Outside of the US, the term coach refers to another person who is only responsible for running the training program, while team strategy is handled by a manager.

Above, Chelsea coach Dave Sexton uses miniature soccer to demonstrate tactics to manager Tommy Docherty and the Chelsea players in 1963.

THE MANAGER

While one person handles both training and management in US soccer, outside the US an additional role called "manager" exists. The manager works with the coach, plans the tactics, motivates players before a game, decides what new players to buy, and actually picks the team.

During training sessions the coach will show the team the lessons they can learn from their previous performances.

THE PHYSICAL THERAPIST

Whenever players are injured during a soccer match, they will be attended to by a physical therapist. In addition to seeing to the players' needs on the field, he or she helps players regain match fitness after broken legs, pulled muscles, sprains, tendon troubles, or cartilage problems. The physical therapist also determines whether players are sufficiently recovered enough to play again.

During a game, the physical therapist has to be ready to run onto the field at any time to attend to injured players. Above, a physical therapist uses a spray to alleviate the pain of a leg injury.

Injured players follow a series of exercises specified by the physical therapist to regain fitness.

Left, Silvio Berlusconi (owner) and right, Fabio Capello (coach) celebrate after AC Milan wins the Italian League in 1994.

THE CHAIRPERSON

The chairperson, or president, is the head of the whole soccer club. He or she and a board of directors are responsible for the financial arrangements at the club, and work in close consultation with the manager to decide how much money is available to buy new players. Chairpersons are usually business people or celebrities, although occasionally they are former soccer players.

Rain stops play! Ground staff attempts to clear floodwaters at Stamford Bridge, England in 1965. Chelsea's game was canceled.

After each match the team's uniforms have to be washed and made ready for the next game.

EQUIPMENT MANAGER

The person who organizes the team's uniforms has to make sure that for every game each player has a full set of clean shirts, shorts, socks, and shoes. Sometimes players in a club's youth or reserve team help get the gear ready.

THE GROUND STAFF

At the beginning of the season many soccer fields look like smooth green carpets, the grass freshly mown, and not a divot in sight. As the season progresses and more games are played on the surface, it is the job of the ground staff to make sure that the field remains in good condition. A poor field results in greater likelihood of injury and second-rate performances. Synthetic surfaces are still relatively rare, especially outside the US, so the ground staff's role remains of crucial importance.

Maintenance of the field is essential, and a team of people is responsible for keeping weeds at bay and limiting the damage caused by the environment and matches. This groundskeeper is using a hot-air blower to clear the field.

8:30 AM Ground staff opens up. Field inspected.

9:00 AM General office and ticket office open.

9:15 AM Match programs delivered.

9:30 AM Home team uniforms laid out.
10:30 AM Refreshment stands stocked up.

BEHIND THE SCENES ON MATCH DAY

IN ADDITION TO THE 22 players, referee, and two assistant referees, behind the scenes a whole army of people is needed to make today's soccer matches happen. Work starts many hours before the game kicks off and continues well after the game ends and the fans go home. The timetable described here is very generalized, and around the world some things are done slightly differently, but it does give an insight into the preparation involved in putting on a soccer match for a major club team.

11:00 AM Catering staff begins to prepare meals for sponsors and guests.

12:00 PM *Match officials arrive. Examine field to make sure it is playable.*

12:15 PM *Match staff arrives: turnstile operators, ushers, and program sellers.*

12:45 PM *Police and paramedics arrive. Stadium manager briefs police, ushers, and security staff. Closed-circuit TV monitoring system switched on.*

1:00 PM *Home team players arrive.*

1:15 PM *Turnstiles opened.*

1:45 PM *Away team arrives.*

2:00 PM *Fans begin to arrive.*

2:15 PM *Teams warm up on field, then return to locker rooms.*

2:30 PM *Coaches give list of players in teams to referee. Prematch entertainment begins.*

2:45 PM *Coaches give prematch team talk.*

2:55 PM *Referees lead teams out.*

2:55 PM Coach, manager, physical therapist, and substitutes take their places at side of field.

3:00 PM Match kicks off.

3:45 PM Halftime. Ground staff checks field.

4:00 PM Second half starts.

4:05 PM Security firm collects takings.

4:45 PM Game ends. Fans begin to leave.

4:50 PM TV coverage ends after postmatch interviews.

4:55 PM Police and ushers debriefed. Ground staff checks field.

5:00 PM Players clean up. Uniforms are sorted for washing.

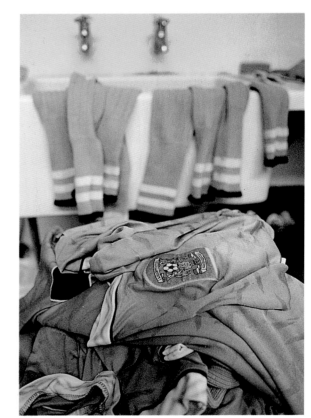

5:05 PM Catering staff clears up. Garbage cleared from stands.

5:30 PM Teams leave.

5:45 PM Match staff leaves.

6:30 PM Stadium empty. Commercial manager or catering manager locks up.

1882 English Cup Final team, Blackburn Rovers

GREAT TEAMS

Soccer is about eleven people working together like a

well-oiled machine. Over the years, there have been

many great teams that have produced some dazzling

displays of soccer and won the world's most

prestigious trophies along the way.

Note: Team factfiles list the top goalscorers and most capped players for each national team (with years they played), plus a summary of each team's major achievements.

Confederacao Brasileira de Futebol, founded in 1914

BRAZIL

MOST PEOPLE AGREE THAT there has never been a greater soccer team than the Brazilian World Cup winning team of 1970. Their sublime, flowing soccer left opponents reeling and soccer fans around the globe in ecstasy. Although there has never been another team like them, Brazilian teams before and since have always been full of flair and invention. With dazzling displays of ball control and some amazing free kicks, they captivate audiences the world over. Brazil is the 1994 world-champion team and is considered the most successful international team ever.

HISTORY
Migrant British workers introduced soccer to Brazil at the end of the nineteenth century. Due to the size of the country, it wasn't until 1971 that a national League was set up.

Romario holds the World Cup trophy after Brazil's 1994 victory over Italy.

Brazil has produced some of the world's greatest players, such as

Djalma Santos, Garrincha, Pele, Jairzinho, Romario, and Ronaldo to

name but a few. Their brilliant dribbling and

"awesome finishing"

have brought joy to millions.

Brazil with the Swedish flag after winning the World Cup in 1958 against Sweden in Stockholm

AN UNPARALLELED SUCCESS
Brazil is the only national team to have played in every World Cup. They have won the tournament a record four times in 1958, 1962, 1970, and 1994. They were runners-up to Uruguay in 1950, and were third-placed in 1938 and 1978. Brazil has also won the South American Championship on five occasions.

WINNING IN 1994
The key to Brazil's 1994 World Cup success was the partnership of Romario and Bebeto. Romario either scored or helped to create 10 of the 11 goals Brazil gained on its way to the Final. The Final itself ended goalless, and Brazil became the first team to win the World Cup on a penalty shoot-out.

Brazil's team colors: yellow shirts, blue shorts, and blue socks

PELE
The greatest player ever to pull on a Brazil shirt was Pele, who made his debut for Brazil in 1957 at the age of 16, in a match against Argentina.

Factfile

Top Goalscorers
1. Pele 77 (1957-71)
2. Zico 54 (1971-86)
3. Jairzinho 38 (1963-82)

Most Appearances
1. Djalma Santos 100 (1952-68)
2. Gilmar 95 (1953-69)
3. Roberto Rivelino 94 (1965-78)

1958 World Cup
Brazil beat Sweden 5-2 in the Final.

1962 World Cup
Brazil defeated Czechoslovakia 3-1 in the Final.

1970 World Cup
Brazil beat Italy 4-1 in the Final.

1994 World Cup
Brazil and Italy tied 0-0 in the Final. Brazil won 3-2 on penalties.

PLAYING TO THE BEAT OF A DRUM
Brazilians are among the most colorful and enthusiastic soccer fans in the world. The whistles and rhythm of samba drums create a party atmosphere when the national teams or top club teams, such as Santos, Flamengo, Fluminense, São Paulo, and Vasco da Gama, take to the field.

Brazil's Ronaldo playing for Barcelona in 1996

GARRINCHA
Known as "Little Bird," Garrincha played in both the 1958 and 1962 World Cup winning teams. His skillful footwork destroyed many a defense as England found in the 1962 finals tournament when he scored twice against them.

RONALDO
Ronaldo is perhaps the world's most exciting player today. In 1997 aged 20, the Brazilian striker scored the winning goal in Barcelona's European Cup Winners' Cup victory over Paris Saint-Germain.

In 1997, Brazil won the Copa America for the fifth time. Who did they beat in the Final?

Deutscher Fussball-Bund, founded in 1900

GERMANY

Germany's team colors:
white shirts, black shorts,
and white socks

GERMANY IS BY FAR Europe's most successful soccer–playing nation. The German team has reached the World Cup Final six times, more than any other team, and has won on three occasions. In 1996, Germany became European champions for the third time. With the legendary Franz Beckenbauer and the great goalscorer Gerd Müller, German club team Bayern Munich dominated European soccer in the 1970s. German reunification in 1990 gave the national team a greater pool of players.

HISTORY
Soccer began in Germany in the 1880s. By 1898, regional leagues had been set up with the winners of each league competing to be national champions. Postwar Germany was split into East and West, and in 1963, a single national League, the Bundesliga, was formed in West Germany.

WOLFGANG OVERATH
Overath was a midfielder and played all his domestic games with the West German club Köln. He had a key role in the West German World Cup teams of 1966, 1970, and 1974.

"Tactical and determined,"

German teams can play a very quick and exciting passing game. They also possess extremely skillful players.

Overath (left) and Müller (right) celebrate W. Germany's 2-1 victory over Holland in the 1974 World Cup Final.

WORLD CHAMPIONS ...
West Germany first won the World Cup in 1954, beating Hungary 3-2 after being two goals down. They won again in 1974, beating Holland 2-1, and in 1990, beating Argentina 1- They were runners-up to England in 1966, (losing 4-2), to Ital in 1982, (losing 3-1), and to Argentina in 1986, (losing 3-2).

... AND EUROPEAN CHAMPIONS!
Germany is the only team to have won the European Championship more than once. They are the 1996 holders, having beaten the Czech Republic 2-1, and Belgium 2-1 in 1980, and the Soviet Union 3-0 in 1972.

GERD MÜLLER

Known as "Der Bomber," Gerd Müller (right) was lethal in front of a goal. He is Germany's highest goalscorer of all time, with a staggering 68 goals in 62 internationals. He also scored 365 times in the German League for Bayern Munich, a record that still stands today.

BAYERN MUNICH

With 14 League titles to its name and European Cup wins in 1974, 1975, and 1976, Bayern Munich is Germany's most successful club. With Beckenbauer as manager, they also won the UEFA Cup in 1996.

JÜRGEN KLINSMANN

Loved by fans wherever he goes, Jürgen Klinsmann raised the 1996 European Championship trophy as captain of his country's team. A prolific goalscorer, he scored 15 goals in Bayern Munich's 1996 UEFA Cup campaign – a record for goals scored in a single European club competition.

Müller (above) was a powerful center forward with great heading ability and remarkable goal-scoring talent.

Factfile

(Including W. Germany)

Top Goalscorers
1. Gerd Müller 68 (1966-74)
2. Rudi Völler 47 (1982-94)
3. Karl-Heinz Rummenigge 45 (1976-86)

Most Appearances
1. Lothar Matthäus 122 (1980-94)
2. Franz Beckenbauer 103 (1965-77)
3. Jürgen Klinsmann 100 (1987-)

1974 World Cup
W. Germany beat Holland 2-1 in the Final.

1990 World Cup
W. Germany defeated Argentina 1-0 in the Final.

1996 European Championship
Germany beat the Czech Republic 2-1 in the Final.

Jürgen Klinsmann in action in the European Championship in 1996. He is one of Germany's greatest strikers, and scored three goals during the championship.

FRANZ BECKENBAUER

One of the world's greatest players, Beckenbauer captained West Germany to World Cup glory in 1974 and was their winning manager in the 1990 World Cup.

Who was the last German to miss a penalty in a penalty shoot-out in any game?

Federazione Italiana Giuoco Calcio, founded in 1898

ITALY

AT THE INTERNATIONAL LEVEL, Italy has appeared in five World Cup Finals, winning three times, and has won the European Championship once, in 1968. Without a doubt, Italians play some of the best soccer in the world, but in the past they have been criticized for playing too defensively. The top league division in Italy, Serie A, is generally regarded as the best in the world, with many of the world's biggest stars, huge attendances, and skillful, exciting matches. Italian club teams, notably Juventus and AC Milan, have won many European titles.

Italy's team colors: blue shirts, white shorts, and blue socks

HISTORY
The first Italian League champion was Genoa in 1898. However, they only had to play three games to win the title. It wasn't until 1929 that a single national league was introduced and the number of games played greatly increased.

PAOLO ROSSI
A star of the 1978 World Cup, Rossi was the top scorer in the 1982 World Cup with six goals, including the first goal against West Germany.

PAOLO MALDINI
Considered to be the best defender in the world, Maldini is the most capped player of the current Italian squad.

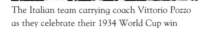
The Italian team carrying coach Vittorio Pozzo as they celebrate their 1934 World Cup win

THE GLORY YEARS
The 1930s were the greatest years for Italian soccer. In this entire decade, Italy lost only nine games. The acclaimed coach, Vittorio Pozzo, led them to victory in the World Cup in 1934 and 1938, and at the Olympics in 1936. Their postwar success included winning the European Championship in 1968 and the World Cup for a third time in 1982.

Zoff raising the World Cup trophy in 1982

DINO ZOFF
The legendary goalkeeper Zoff became the oldest player to raise the World Cup when he captained the winning team of 1982 at the age of 40. He went on to manage top Italian teams Juventus and Lazio.

⚽ Which team shocked the world by beating Italy 1-0 in the World Cup finals of 1966? ⚽

Marco Tardelli scores against W. Germany in the 1982 World Cup Final.

UNDER PRESSURE

Italy's players often seem under greater pressure to succeed than any others. But when they do experience victory, their joy is unbridled. Above, Marco Tardelli expresses his elation on scoring Italy's second goal in the 1982 World Cup Final.

Italian soccer can be both exhilarating and frustrating, but at its best it is

"creative and penetrating."

Pietro Vierchowod for Juventus and George Weah for AC Milan in 1996

JUVENTUS AND AC MILAN

The most successful Italian clubs are Juventus of Turin and AC Milan. Between them they have won 13 major European trophies and have topped Serie A 39 times.

CATENACCIO

If you don't concede a goal you can't lose became the philosophy of Italian soccer in the 1960s and 1970s. Tight defense was the order of the day and free-flowing soccer suffered. Thankfully, more recently all that has changed as shown by Arrigo Sacchi's breathtaking Milan team of the late 1980s and early 1990s.

AC Milan fans at the 1989 European Cup Final

FRANCO BARESI

The tough man of Italian soccer, Baresi was both a solid defender and a very skillful player. Throughout his domestic career, he played for club team AC Milan, with whom he clocked up more than 600 appearances.

FERVENT FANS

Italian supporters are some of the most passionate in soccer. Their constant chanting and firing of colorful flares ensures that the atmosphere in Italian games rarely drops below boiling point.

Factfile

Top Goalscorers
1. Luigi Riva 35 (1965-74)
2. Giuseppe Meazza 33 (1930-39)
3. Silvio Piola 30 (1935-52)

Most Appearances
1. Dino Zoff 112 (1968-83)
2. Giacinto Facchetti 94 (1963-77)
3. Marco Tardelli 81 (1976-85) Franco Baresi 81 (1982-94)

1934 World Cup
Italy beat Czechoslovakia 2-1 in the Final.

1938 World Cup
Italy defeated Hungary 4-2 in the Final.

1968 European Championship
Italy beat Yugoslavia 2-0 to become European Champions.

1982 World Cup
Italy defeated W. Germany 3-1 in the Final.

 What does "catenaccio" mean?

ARGENTINA

Asociacion del Futbol Argentino, founded in 1893

ALONGSIDE BRAZIL, ARGENTINA is the other South American giant of world soccer. Their most renowned player is the legendary Diego Maradona. He led Argentina to its second World Cup victory in 1986. They first won in 1978. They have reached the Final of four World Cups in total and have won the South American Championship (Copa America) no less than 14 times.

Argentina's team colors: sky-blue-and-white striped shirts, black shorts, and white socks

In 1993, Argentina defeated first-time entrant Mexico in the Copa America to become champions for the fourteenth time.

HISTORY
Argentina is the second oldest soccer-playing nation after Britain, and was introduced to the game by Britain in 1865. In 1901, Argentina played in the first international match to be held outside Britain. It was against Uruguay, who was to become their arch rival.

DIEGO MARADONA
Diego Armando Maradona (left) was one of the greatest players the world has ever seen. Though not always on his best behavior, when the only thing on his mind was soccer, he was breathtaking.

Osvaldo Ardiles

Argentina's style is very much in the

Latin mold, with the emphasis on skillful,

"attack-minded play."

WORLD CUP WINS
It was second-time lucky for Argentina in 1978 when, after losing the 1930 Final 4-2 to Uruguay, they won the World Cup on home soil, beating Holland 3-1. Eight years later in Mexico, they were champions again after defeating West Germany 3-2. Argentina narrowly missed holding on to the trophy in 1990, losing 1-0 to West Germany.

OSVALDO ARDILES
A tricky, attacking midfielder, Ardiles was one of Argentina's most successful exports. After helping his country win the 1978 World Cup, he was transferred to English club Tottenham Hotspur for £300,000 ($480,000).

⚽ Argentina and Uruguay have played each other more times than any other two countries. ⚽
What was the score when they first met in 1901?

RIVER PLATE

The year 1986 was to go down in history for Argentina's most successful club team River Plate. They won the Argentinian League, the Inter-American Cup, the Copa Libertadores, and the World Club Cup.

Zamora for River Plate in the white shirt with red stripe

Factfile

Top Goalscorers
1. Gabriel Batistuta 33 (1991-)
   Diego Maradona 33 (1977-94)
2. Luis Artime 24 (1960-68)
3. Daniel Passarella 23
   (1976-85)

Most Appearances
1. Oscar Ruggeri 98 (1983-95)
2. Diego Maradona 90 (1974-94)
3. Amerigo Gallego 71 (1975-82)

1978 World Cup
Argentina beat Holland 3-1 in the Final.

1986 World Cup
Argentina defeated W. Germany 3-2 in the Final.

Striker Mario Kempes played in three World Cups: 1974, 1978, and 1982.

MARIO KEMPES

As an aggressive young striker, Mario Kempes got his first taste of World Cup soccer in the 1974 tournament. Top scorer of the 1978 World Cup with six goals, Kempes scored two of those in the Final itself, making him the most recent player to score more than one goal in a World Cup Final. Kempes also appeared in the 1982 finals tournament, but his form of 1978 was never recaptured.

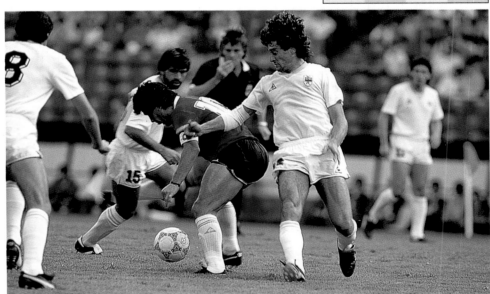

Argentina against Uruguay in 1986

THE OLD ENEMY

Argentina's greatest rival is Uruguay. The two South American teams have faced each other 182 times, making this game the most played international match in the world.

Who did Argentina beat in their semifinal in the first ever World Cup in 1930?

FRANCE

Fédération Française de Football, founded in 1918

France's team colors: blue shirts, white shorts, and red socks

WORLD SOCCER OWES a huge debt of gratitude to the French, for it was they who first came up with the idea of a World Cup competition. Sadly, they have never been champions themselves, though they have been semifinalists on three occasions, and Frenchman Just Fontaine holds the record for the number of goals scored in a World Cup finals tournament. France tasted success in 1984 when a team packed with stars, such as the great Platini, Giresse, Tigana, and Battiston, won the European Championship.

France celebrating Platini's goal in the 1984 European Championship Final

HISTORY

Rugby was by far the most popular French sport in the latter half of the last century, and initially, soccer clubs were offshoots of rugby clubs. It wasn't until 1892 that the first French clubs devoted entirely to soccer were formed.

Just Fontaine

At their best France plays exciting, *"flowing football,"* as epitomized by the 1984 team that won the European Championship and was a joy to watch.

JUST FONTAINE

Fontaine had played just five times for France before the 1958 World Cup finals. Yet he scored in every one of France's matches. He scored 13 goals, more than anyone has ever scored in one tournament.

DEFEAT IN 1982

In the 1982 World Cup semifinal, a dubious challenge by German goalkeeper Harald Schumacher on defender Battiston went unpunished. It was widely seen as a terrible miscarriage of justice. The French battled hard and at the end of overtime the score was 3-3, but they eventually lost on penalties.

Platini scored in every game of the 1984 European Championship. In the Final, who scored France's other goal in their 2-0 victory against Spain?

VICTORY IN 1984
With the brilliant Michel Platini as captain, France won every game en route to beating Spain 2-0 in the 1984 European Championship Final. Playing in midfield, Michel Platini was a genius with a knack for scoring great goals. Raising the trophy for his country in 1984 was his crowning glory.

Eric Cantona playing for France

ERIC CANTONA
In his six seasons in the English Premier League, Eric Cantona was a championship winner five times. An attacking midfielder for Manchester United and a dominating presence within the team, his skill and vision were second to none. He gave up soccer in 1997 to pursue a career in acting.

Marcel Desailly playing for France in 1995

Michel Platini playing for France in 1984

JEAN PIERRE PAPIN
A natural goalscorer at both club and national level, Papin has always been a danger to his opponents.

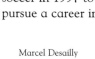

Papin (left) has played for France 54 times. At club level he has played in France, Germany, and Italy.

YOURI DJORKAEFF
One of the new and exciting French players, Djorkaeff's attacking runs and goalscoring ability made him one of his country's stars in the 1996 European Championship.

MARCEL DESAILLY
A hugely talented defender, Desailly (above) was very influential in helping France to reach the semifinals of the European Championship in 1996. He won a European Cup medal with club team Olympique Marseille in 1993, and the following year he won another playing for AC Milan.

Factfile
Top Goalscorers
1. Michel Platini 41 (1976-87)
2. Jean-Pierre Papin 30 (1986-)
3. Just Fontaine 27 (1956-60)

Most Appearances
1. Manuel Amoros 82 (1982-92)
2. Maxime Bossis 76 (1976-86)
3. Michel Platini 72 (1976-87)

1958 World Cup
France was knocked out by Brazil 5-2 in the semifinals.

1982 World Cup
France tied 3-3 with W. Germany in the semifinals after overtime, but lost 5-4 on penalties.

1984 European Championship
France beat Spain 2-0 in the Final.

1986 World Cup
France were beaten by W. Germany 2-0 in the semifinals.

Koninklijke Nederlandsche Voetbalbond,
founded in 1889

HISTORY

Formed in 1889, the Dutch FA is the third oldest in Europe. The national League however, was formed comparatively late in 1957, when professionalism was introduced.

HOLLAND

HOLLAND IS PROBABLY the greatest team never to have been crowned world champions. The national team reached the semifinals of four consecutive Olympics: 1908, 1912, 1920, and 1924. In the mid-1970s they reached two World Cup Finals, narrowly losing on both occasions. In 1988, Holland finally won a major title, the European Championship.

Holland's team colors: orange shirt, white shorts, and orange socks

1988 European Championship team

Ruud Gullit scored the opening goal in the 1988 European Championship Final

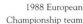

RUUD GULLIT

With his distinctive hairstyle and magnificent skills, Ruud Gullit stood out on the soccer field in more ways than one. In 1988, he raised the European Championship trophy as captain of Holland.

The powerful trio in action: Van Basten, Rijkaard, and Gullit

TOP TEAMS

Dutch clubs have always had great success in nurturing the talents of young soccer players. This is one reason why clubs such as PSV Eindhoven, Ajax, and Feyenoord have done so well in European competitions. Ajax, for example, produced Johan Cruyff, Dennis Bergkamp, Marco Van Basten, and Frank Rijkaard – four of Holland's all-time greats.

  Who scored Holland's second goal when they won the 1988 European Championship Final?

THOSE WORLD CUPS

On the way to their 2-1 defeat in the 1974 World Cup Final, Holland scored 14 goals and conceded only one. In the Final, Neeskens for Holland scored from the penalty spot before any of the West German players had touched the ball. It was the fastest goal ever in a World Cup Final. In the 1978 Final, the Dutch managed to force the game into overtime before they were defeated by Argentina.

Holland's new style of soccer in the 1974 World Cup had a profound effect, since every outfield player could function in any position. This style of play became known as

"total soccer."

Cruyff brought down by Hoeness for a penalty in the 1974 World Cup Final

JOHAN CRUYFF

Cruyff's great ball skills could single-handedly unlock an opponent's defense. He captained Holland in the 1974 World Cup finals and won three European Cups with Ajax.

Dennis Bergkamp in the 1994 World Cup

EUROPEAN CHAMPIONS

The 1988 European Championship gave Holland the trophy they deserved. In Ruud Gullit, Frank Rijkaard, and Marco Van Basten, a new set of Dutch stars emerged. By beating West Germany 2-1 in the semifinals, Holland also found consolation for the defeat in the 1974 World Cup Final.

MARCO VAN BASTEN

After scoring 128 league goals for Ajax, in 1987 Marco Van Basten joined Italian club AC Milan, with whom he won the European Cup in 1989 and 1990. He was at his peak during the 1988 European Championship. An ankle injury spoiled the later years of Van Basten's career.

Van Basten in the 1990 World Cup

Factfile

Top Goalscorers
1. Faas Wilkes 35 (1946-61)
2. Abe Lenstra 33 (1940-59)
   Johan Cruyff 33 (1966-77)
3. Dennis Bergkamp 32 (1990-)

Most Appearances
1. Ruud Krol 83 (1969-83)
2. Ronald Koeman 78 (1983-94)
3. Frank Rijkaard 73 (1981-94)

1974 World Cup
Holland reached the Final only to be beaten 2-1 by W. Germany.

1978 World Cup
Holland made it to the Final again, but this time was beaten by Argentina 3-1.

1988 European Championship
Holland beat the Soviet Union 2-0 in the Final.

DENNIS BERGKAMP

Bergkamp (left) is known as the "Ice Man" because of his cool temperament and composed, clinical playing style. He has made more than 40 appearances for his country and scored more than 20 international goals.

The English Football Association, founded in 1863

ENGLAND

England's team colors: white shirts, blue shorts, and white socks

THE GAME AS WE KNOW IT today has been played in England longer than anywhere else. Probably for that reason, the English have often considered themselves to be the best in the world. While their performances have rarely justified that claim, when they won the World Cup on home soil in 1966, few could argue with it. The English Premier League is widely regarded as the hardest in the world to win, and, with the current influx of foreign superstars, it can also lay claim to being one of the world's most prestigious championships. Club teams such as Manchester United, Liverpool, and Chelsea are famous around the globe, and over the years, England has produced some great players, such as Stanley Matthews, Bobby Charlton, Bobby Moore, Alan Shearer, and Paul Gascoigne.

HISTORY
In 1848, Cambridge University drew up the first rules for soccer. In 1863, the newly formed English Football Association established a set of rules. The English FA Cup began in 1872 and became crucial to the game's development in England.

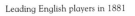

Leading English players in 1881

Bobby Moore celebrating England's World Cup win in 1966

WORLD CHAMPIONS IN 1966
Three goals by Geoff Hurst (below, second from left) ensured England's finest hour when they defeated West Germany 4-2 at Wembley Stadium to win the 1966 World Cup. Geoff Hurst is the only player to score a hat trick in a World Cup Final.

TWO GREAT BOBBIES
Bobby Moore captained England to World Cup victory in 1966 and is probably the greatest defender the country has ever produced. On the same victorious team was Bobby Charlton, who has scored more goals for England than anyone else.

Bobby Charlton

Soccer in England has always been *"fast and* and many consider the English Premier League to be the most exciting in the world.

TOP ENGLISH CLUBS

Manchester United became the first English team to win the European Cup in 1968 and more recently they became the only team to win the English League and Cup "double" twice. Liverpool is the most successful club in English soccer with 18 championship wins, four European Cup victories, and two UEFA Cup triumphs.

Peter Schmeichel and Ole Gunnar Solskjaer for Manchester United, against Stan Collymore for Liverpool in 1997

David Seaman saves Nadal's penalty in a 1996 European Championship quarterfinal against Spain. England won in a penalty shoot-out.

GREAT GOALKEEPERS

England has always produced very fine goalkeepers. In Gordon Banks the England team probably had the best goalkeeper ever, and Peter Shilton (below) is their most capped player. David Seaman (above) is regarded by some as the best keeper in the world at the moment.

Factfile

Top Goalscorers
1. Bobby Charlton 49 (1958-70)
2. Gary Lineker 48 (1984-92)
3. Jimmy Greaves 44 (1959-67)

Most Appearances
1. Peter Shilton 125 (1970-90)
2. Bobby Moore 108 (1962-73)
3. Bobby Charlton 106 (1958-70)

1966 World Cup
England defeated W. Germany 4-2 in the Final.

1990 World Cup
England was beaten 4-3 on penalties in the semifinals by W. Germany.

1997 Tournoi de France
England won this four-nation contest on points.

ALAN SHEARER

Alan Shearer became the world's most expensive player when Newcastle paid Blackburn Rovers £15 million ($24 million) for him in 1996. A prolific goalscorer, he is the first man to have scored 100 goals in the English Premier League, and he was the top scorer in the 1996 European Championship tournament with five goals.

physical"

Alan Shearer in a first round group match against Holland in the 1996 European Championship. England won 4-1.

Peter Shilton (above) playing for England in 1989

Gascoigne received his second yellow card in the 1990 World Cup semifinals, so had England reached the Final, he would have been unable to play.

PAUL GASCOIGNE

Possessing excellent close ball control, superb long-range passing skills, and an ability to conjure up scoring opportunities, Paul Gascoigne is the most gifted English player of his generation. He was outstanding during the 1990 World Cup, and was a key player in the 1996 European Championship.

Which player made England's fastest ever World Cup goal when he scored against France in 1982 after just 27 seconds?

URUGUAY

Asociacion Uruguaya de Futbol, founded in 1900

PENAROL
Uruguay's most successful club is Penarol. In 1982, they became the first team to win the World Club Cup three times, beating English team Aston Villa 2-0.

Uruguay's team colors: blue shirts, black shorts, and black socks

WITH THEIR OLYMPIC-CHAMPION national team, Uruguay hosted the first World Cup in 1930 and, to the delight of the home crowd, they won the trophy. Uruguay won the trophy again in 1950, this time in Brazil, becoming the first South American team to win two World Cups. Although the national team has not been in the World Cup reckoning in recent years, they have won the South American Championship 14 times – a record matched only by Argentina.

The 1928 Olympic Games Final was a 1-1 tie. Uruguay won the rematch.

OLYMPIC CHAMPIONS
South American soccer players entered the Olympic Games for the first time in 1924. Uruguay defeated Switzerland 3-0 in the Final. Uruguay won the gold medal again in Holland in 1928, defeating Holland, Germany, and Italy, before finally beating their greatest rivals, Argentina 2-1.

Uruguay's captain (left) and Argentina's captain (right) with the referee and linesmen in the 1928 Olympics.

Lorenzo Fernandez, Pedro Cea, and Hector Scarone celebrate Uruguay's victory in the first World Cup Final in 1930.

WORLD CHAMPIONS
In the first World Cup Final in 1930, host Uruguay defeated Argentina 4-2 in front of 93,000 people in Montevideo. In 1950 in Brazil, they shocked local fans when they defeated a much-favored home team 2-1 to become world champions for a second time.

Uruguay's goalkeeper, Maspoli, failed to save this shot by Brazil's Friaca in the 1950 World Cup Final. However, Uruguay went on to win 2-1.

Factfile

Top Goalscorers
1. Hector Scarone 29 (1917-30)
2. Angel Romano 28 (1911-27)
3. Omar Miguez 26 (1950-58)

Most Appearances
1. Rodolfo Rodriguez 78 (1976-86)
2. Enzo Francescoli 70 (1983-97)
3. Angel Romano 69 (1911-27)

1924 Olympics
Uruguay beat Switzerland 3-0 in the Final.

1928 Olympics
Uruguay tied 1-1 in the Final against Argentina, then won the rematch 2-1.

1930 World Cup
Hosts Uruguay defeated Argentina 4-2 in the Final.

1950 World Cup
Uruguay beat host Brazil 2-1 in the Final.

Who was the captain of Uruguay and the first player to raise the World Cup trophy in 1930?

HUGARY

Magyar Labdarugo Szovetseg, founded 1901

Hungary's team colors: red shirts, white shorts, and green socks

BETWEEN MAY 1950 AND JULY 1954, Hungary lost only one match. Unfortunately, that was the 1954 World Cup Final. There is no doubt however, that the 1954 Hungarian team was one of the greatest teams of all time. They were known as the "Magical Magyars" and in Ferenc Puskas and Sandor Kocsis they had a deadly striking partnership. Hungary achieved Olympic victory in 1952, 1964, and 1968, and in 1953 they became the first foreign team to beat England on English soil.

Hungary players line up before the match against England at Wembley in 1953.

OLYMPIC CHAMPIONS
Hungary have been victorious at the Olympics three times. Interestingly, on each occasion they have defeated fellow East European teams to take the gold medal, beating Yugoslavia 2-0 in 1952, Czechoslovakia 2-1 in 1964, and Bulgaria 4-1 in 1968.

The captains of each winning team with their medals at the 1964 Olympics. Hungary won gold, Czechoslovakia silver, and West Germany bronze.

Factfile

Top Goalscorers
1. Ferenc Puskas 82 (1945-56)
2. Sandor Kocsis 75 (1948-56)
3. Imre Schlosser 58 (1906-27)

Most Appearances
1. Jozsef Bozsik 100 (1947-62)
2. Laszlo Fazekas 92 (1968-83)
3. Gyula Grosics 86 (1947-62)

1952 Olympics
Hungary defeated Yugoslavia 2-0 in the Final.

1954 World Cup
Hungary was defeated 3-2 in the Final by W. Germany.

1964 Olympics
Hungary defeated Czechoslovakia 2-1 in the Final. They won the Olympics again in 1968, beating Bulgaria 4-1 in the Final.

WORLD RUNNERS-UP
After beating West Germany 8-3 in a group match, Hungary was confident of winning when the two teams met in the 1954 World Cup Final. Incredibly, Hungary squandered a two-goal lead and allowed the Germans to win 3-2.

W. Germany scoring their first goal against Hungary in the 1954 World Cup Final

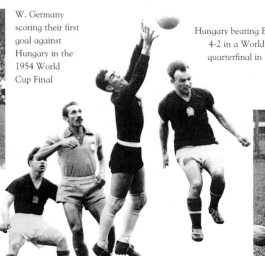

Hungary beating Brazil 4-2 in a World Cup quarterfinal in 1954

FERENC PUSKAS
One of the world's greatest players, Puskas, who had a deadly left foot, is still Hungary's top goalscorer. Puskas was Hungary's captain and, later, was able to play for Spain due to residency there.

Puskas playing for Hungary in 1953

 Who was the last team to defeat Hungary before their unbeaten run leading up to the 1954 World Cup Final?

49

All Russian Football Union, founded in 1912

RUSSIA

RUSSIA, FORMERLY KNOWN as the Soviet Union, has always fielded strong teams that are difficult to beat. In 1956, the Soviets became Olympic champions for the first time and four years later they were the first winners of the European Championship. On both occasions, the legendary Lev Yashin was in the goal. They have also reached three other European Championship Finals, finishing as runners-up each time, and in 1988 they again won Olympic gold. World Cup glory however, has eluded them and a semifinal appearance in 1966 has been their best performance.

Russia's team colors: white shirts, blue shorts, and red socks

1960 European champions

EUROPEAN FINALISTS
After winning the first European Championship in 1960, the Soviets lost 2-1 to Spain in the 1964 Final. They also lost 3-0 to West Germany in the 1972 Final, and 2-0 to Holland in the Final of the 1988 championship.

Lev Yashin making a save in the 1956 Olympic Final

LEV YASHIN
Considered by many to be the greatest goalkeeper ever, Yashin played 78 times for his country in a career that ran from 1954 to 1970. Yashin was famous for stopping shots that no other goalkeeper could reach.

Factfile

Top Goalscorers
1. Oleg Blokhin 39 (1972-88)
2. Oleg Protasov 29 (1984-92)
3. Valentin Ivanov 26 (1955-65)

Most Appearances
1. Oleg Blokhin 109 (1972-88)
2. Rinat Dasayev 94 (1979-90)
3. Albert Shesternev 89 (1961-71)

1960 European Championship
The Soviet Union beat Yugoslavia 2-1 in the Final of the first European Championship held in France.

1988 Olympics
The Soviet Union beat Brazil 2-1 in the Final. They had previously won the Olympics in 1956, beating Yugoslavia 1-0.

Brazil's Farias and Souza clash with Ketachvili of the Soviet Union in the 1988 Olympic Final.

OLYMPIC CHAMPIONS
In front of 120,000 spectators at the Melbourne Cricket Ground, the Soviets beat Yugoslavia to become champions at the 1956 Melbourne Olympics. In 1988, they won gold again at the Seoul Olympics, this time beating Brazil 2-1 in the Final.

The Soviet Union at the 1962 World Cup finals tournament in Chile. They were defeated 2-1 by Chile in the quarterfinals.

 Aside from Lev Yashin, who is the only other Soviet Union player who has been named European Soccer Player of the Year?

SPAIN

Spain's team colors: red shirts, blue shorts, and blue socks

Real Federation Española de Futbol, founded in 1913

The triumphant Spanish team with their manager, Villalonga, in 1964

IN REAL MADRID and Barcelona, Spain has two of the greatest club teams in the world. Between them they have appeared in 27 European competition Finals, winning on 16 occasions. The national team, however, has found success harder to come by. Their only major trophy has been the European Championship in 1964 and they have never reached a World Cup semifinal. More recently, the Under-23 team won the 1992 Olympic tournament. But with the passion the Spanish have for the game, they will always be a force to be reckoned with.

Factfile

Top Goalscorers
1. Emilio Butragueño 26 (1984-92)
2. Alfredo Di Stefano 23 (1957-61)
3. Miguel Gonzalez 'Michel' 21 (1985-93)
   Julio Salinas 21 (1986-96)

Most Appearances
1. Andoni Zubizarreta 110 (1983-)
2. Jose Antonio Camacho 81 (1975-88)
3. Rafael Gordillo 75 (1978-88)

1964 European Championship
Spain beat the Soviet Union 2-1 in the Final.

1992 Olympics
Spain defeated Poland 3-2 in the Final.

EUROPEAN CHAMPIONS
Spain won the European Championship in 1964 by beating the Soviet Union 2-1 in front of 105,000 people in Madrid's Bernabeu Stadium. Their two goals came from Pereda and Marcelino.

Luis Suarez as a player in 1961 (above) and as the manager of Spain in 1990 (left)

LUIS SUAREZ
Suarez is probably the greatest Spanish soccer player of all time. His success came in the 1960s with club team Internazionale of Italy. He went on to be a coach and a manager, and took Spain to the 1990 World Cup.

The victorious Under-23 1992 Olympic team

OLYMPIC CHAMPIONS
Once again on home soil, this time in Barcelona's Nou Camp Stadium in front of 95,000 people, Spain's talented young team won the 1992 Olympics by defeating Poland 3-2.

REAL MADRID AND BARCELONA
Fierce rivals, these two teams have dominated the Spanish domestic game for years. In particular, the Real Madrid team of the late 1950s, which won the first five European Cup competitions and boasted such great players as Di Stefano and Puskas, will be remembered as one of the greatest teams ever. More recently however, European success has largely eluded Real Madrid, and Barcelona has been the more successful of the two teams.

Real Madrid in 1960 with Alfredo Di Stefano (holding ball) and Ferenc Puskas (front row, second from right)

Zamorano for Real Madrid (left) and Koeman for Barcelona (right) in 1992

 Barcelona and Real Madrid have won numerous Spanish trophies. Which team has won the Spanish Cup more often?

US WOMEN

United States Soccer Federation, founded in 1913

WINNERS OF THE FIRST ever World Cup for women, and the 1996 Olympic champions, there is little doubt that the US women's team is going to be a major team for many years to come. The game in America is being played by more women than ever before, and in Michelle Akers they possess the first true star of the women's game.

US women's team colors: navy shirts, navy shorts, and navy socks (also play in white)

Michelle Akers celebrates Olympic victory in 1996.

Akers clashes with Haugen in 1996.

Factfile

Top Goalscorers
1. Michelle Akers 92 (1985-)
2. Mia Hamm 64 (1987-)
3. Carin Gabarra 53 (1987-96)

Most Appearances
1. Kristine Lilly 124 (1987-)
2. Mia Hamm 123 (1987-)
3. Carin Gabarra 117 (1987-96)

1991 World Cup
The US women's team defeated Norway 2-1 in the Final.

1996 Olympics
The US women's team beat China 2-0 in the Final.

WORLD CHAMPIONS
The United States won all their games on the way to winning the inaugural women's World Cup in China in 1991. In the Final in Guangzhoa, they defeated Norway 2-1.

SEMIFINALISTS IN 1995
The US lost to Norway 1-0 in the semifinals of the 1995 World Cup (right). Norway went on to win the World Cup, beating Germany 2-0 in the Final.

MICHELLE AKERS
Michelle Akers has scored more goals for the US than anyone else, and she was the top goalscorer in the 1991 World Cup tournament with ten goals.

Mia Hamm (right) at the Olympics

OLYMPIC CHAMPIONS
At the Atlanta Games in 1996, the competition was much stiffer than in the 1995 World Cup, but after defeating Norway in the semifinals, the US went on to beat China and take gold.

Against which team did Akers make her debut for the US?

Nigeria Football Association, founded in 1945

NIGERIA

WITH THE EMERGENCE of Africa as a mighty force in world soccer, it was inevitable that before long an African nation would win a major international title. That honor fell to Nigeria when they became Olympic champions in 1996. This much-deserved victory came as no surprise, because Nigeria had finished top of their first round group in the 1994 World Cup. They had also come close to beating eventual finalist Italy in the second round of that tournament. Nigeria has won the African Nations Cup twice, in 1980 and 1994.

Nigeria's team colors: green shirts, green shorts, and green socks

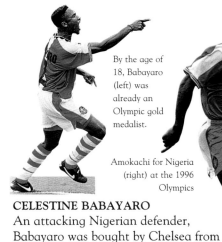

Nigeria's players celebrating their Under-17 World Championship victory in 1985

THE YOUNG PRETENDERS
Nigeria's potential was evident when they won the first ever Under-17 World Championships in 1985, beating West Germany 2-0. They won again in 1993, beating Ghana 2-1.

NWANKWO KANU
As the inspirational captain of Nigeria, Kanu was their highest goalscorer in the 1996 Olympic Games. Almost all the best Nigerian players, including Kanu, have played for European club teams.

Nwankwo Kanu was named African Soccer Player of the Year in 1996.

By the age of 18, Babayaro (left) was already an Olympic gold medalist.

Amokachi for Nigeria (right) at the 1996 Olympics

OLYMPIC CHAMPIONS
One of the strengths of the 1996 Nigerian Olympic team was their ability to come from behind to win. In the semifinals they defeated Brazil after being 3-1 down, and in the Final they were behind to Argentina twice before eventually winning 3-2.

CELESTINE BABAYARO
An attacking Nigerian defender, Babayaro was bought by Chelsea from Belgian team Anderlecht in a £2.25 million ($3.6 million) transfer deal in 1997.

  What is the nickname of the Nigerian team?

TEAMS TO WATCH

Australia in 1997. Many Australian players currently play in Europe and the national team could soon be a World Cup contender.

ONLY SIX DIFFERENT countries have been World Cup champions since the tournament began in 1930. Among them Brazil, Italy, Germany, Argentina, Uruguay, and England have won all fifteen of the finals. However, with national teams the world over becoming stronger all the time, it surely won't be long before new names start appearing at the top of the honor roll. Here are just a few of the countries that might reach those heady heights in years to come.

Ramon Vega and Johann Vogel for Switzerland against Paul Gascoigne for England in the opening match of the 1996 European Championship

SCANDINAVIA AND SWITZERLAND

Denmark is achieving their potential, having won the 1992 European Championship. Sweden reached the semifinals of the same tournament, losing 3-2 to the other eventual finalist Germany. Switzerland qualified for the European Championship for the first time in 1996.

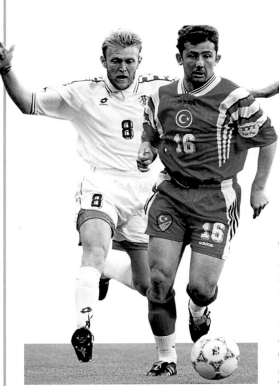

Robert Prosinecki for Croatia, and Sergen Yalcin for Turkey in a match from the 1996 European Championship. Croatia won the game 1-0.

TURKEY

Another country that could achieve success soon is Turkey. At club level, their teams Galatasaray and Fenerbahce are more than holding their own in European competitions, and qualifying for the European Championship in 1996 was a great boost for the national team. To date, Turkey's only appearance in a World Cup finals tournament was in 1954.

An outstanding performance by Bulgaria (in the red-and-white uniforms) against Germany. It brought them a 2-1 victory in the quarterfinals of the 1994 World Cup.

BULGARIA

After knocking out Germany in the 1994 World Cup quarterfinals, Bulgaria was denied a place in the final when they were narrowly defeated by Italy in the semifinals. In Stoichkov, the joint top scorer of the 1994 tournament with six goals, Bulgaria possesses a world-class player.

Cameroon (in the red-and-green uniforms) against South Africa in the African Nations Cup in 1996

CAMEROON

The best bet for a new name on the World Cup trophy must surely come from Africa, with Cameroon high on the list of likely winners. They qualified for the 1982, 1990, and 1994 World Cup finals, and were unlucky to lose 3-2 to England after overtime in the 1990 quarterfinals.

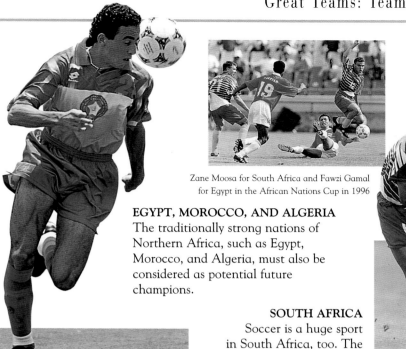

Mohammed Samadi for Morocco in a 1994 World Cup match against Holland

Zane Moosa for South Africa and Fawzi Gamal for Egypt in the African Nations Cup in 1996

EGYPT, MOROCCO, AND ALGERIA

The traditionally strong nations of Northern Africa, such as Egypt, Morocco, and Algeria, must also be considered as potential future champions.

Below, Philemon Massinga of South Africa and Bekhti Karim of Algeria in the African Nations Cup in 1996

SOUTH AFRICA

Soccer is a huge sport in South Africa, too. The South Africans won the 1996 African Nations Cup, beating Tunisia 2-0 in the Final.

SOUTH KOREA, JAPAN, AND CHINA

As co-hosts of the 2002 World Cup, South Korea and Japan have high hopes of glory. The South Koreans have already proved themselves in previous finals and, with Japan's J-League building a base of homegrown players, Japan may also prove to be a strong soccer-playing nation. China is another nation with massive potential. Soccer is growing in popularity there, and their women's team could well bring home their first trophy.

Miura for Japan and Neville for England in the Umbro Cup in 1995

Japan's Kazuyoshi Miura scores a goal against China in the 1996 Asia Games.

Kim Do Hoon for South Korea and Dan Eggen for Norway in 1997

Seo Jung Won for South Korea after scoring the tying point in a 2-2 tie with Spain in the 1994 World Cup

Terry Venables as Australia's coach

AUSTRALIA

The appointment of ex-England coach Terry Venables as the coach for Australia has shown how serious Australia is about improving its status in the game. However, soccer still ranks behind cricket, rugby, and Australian-Rules football in Australian sporting affections.

Pele celebrates his goal in the 1970 World Cup Final.

GREAT PLAYERS

Every once in a while a soccer player comes along

who really stands out. Players such as Pele,

Beckenbauer, or Banks with their breathtaking

skill and ability earn the title of superstar.

PELE

EDSON ARANTES DO NASCIMENTO, or Pele, is the greatest player the world has ever seen. A forward, he played with incredible skill, creativity, and strength. He mesmerized defenders the world over, who, even if they could get near him, often had no way of stopping him. Over the years, many players have been heralded as the "new Pele", but none have been worthy of the title. There was, and always will be, only one Pele.

Pele with the Jules Rimet trophy, 1970

Factfile

Born:	10.23.40 Tres Coracoes, Brazil
Clubs:	**Santos** 1956-74
	1,144 appearances,
	1,090 goals
	New York Cosmos 1975-77
	105 appearances, 55 goals
International Record:	
	Brazil 1957-71
	92 appearances, 77 goals

TEENAGE GLORY

At the age of just 17, Pele scored his first ever World Cup goal in Brazil's 1-0 victory over Wales in the 1958 tournament in Sweden. In the semifinal against France he scored a hat trick, and his two goals in the 5-2 final victory over Sweden gave Brazil the first of their World Cup triumphs.

Pele collects the ball after scoring a penalty for Santos against Vasco da Gama on November 19, 1969. It was his one thousandth goal.

GOALS, GOALS, AND MORE GOALS

Goals were Pele's trademark. His devastating pace and unsurpassed ball control made him a lethal striker. In his professional career, he scored an astounding 1,283 goals in total.

Pele celebrates a goal in the 1970 World Cup Final between Brazil and Italy. He scored Brazil's first goal and assisted two more, contributing to Brazil's 4-1 win.

A spectacular overhead kick from Pele during a 1965 match between Brazil and Belgium

OLDER, WISER, AND JUST AS BRILLIANT

At the age of 29, Pele was at the peak of his powers. He played in every round of the 1970 World Cup. His dummies, shots from the halfway line, and brilliant goals, inspired Brazil's famous World Cup victory.

A NEW CAREER

In 1975, Pele joined the New York Cosmos, helping to establish the popularity of soccer in the United States. He retired in 1977 after the Cosmos had won the NASL Soccer Bowl. Today, Pele remains in the public eye as Brazil's Minister for Sports.

FRANZ BECKENBAUER

Factfile

Born: 9.11.45 Munich, Germany
Clubs: **Bayern Munich** 1962-76
396 appearances, 44 goals
New York Cosmos 1976-83
132 appearances, 23 goals
SV Hamburg 1983-84
28 appearances, 0 goals
International Record:
West Germany 1967-74
103 appearances, 13 goals

GERMANY'S GREATEST PLAYER, Franz Beckenbauer was known as the "Kaiser." From his position as sweeper in the heart of the defense, he was able to influence and organize the whole team. His all-around ability and leadership qualities led him to World Cup glory as a player in 1974, and as manager of West Germany in 1990. As captain of Bayern Munich, he won three European Cup winners' medals and was twice named European Soccer Player of the Year. He then had three NASL Soccer Bowl victories with the New York Cosmos.

ON TOP OF THE WORLD AT LAST
Beckenbauer finally tasted World Cup success as captain of West Germany in their 2-1 victory over the much-favored Dutch team in 1974.

Beckenbauer shoots for a goal in the 1976 European Cup Final between Bayern Munich and Saint-Etienne.

Beckenbauer developed the role of "attacking sweeper," turning defense into attack for Bayern Munich and W. Germany.

A HAT TRICK OF VICTORIES
It was definitely Beckenbauer's year in 1974. With him in the driver's seat, Bayern Munich became the first German team to win the European Cup, beating Atletico Madrid. Bayern then went on to repeat Ajax's three European Cup wins in a row by beating Leeds United in 1975, and Saint-Etienne in 1976.

MANAGING SUCCESS
When West Germany became World Cup champions in 1990, Beckenbauer became the first person to win the World Cup as both captain and manager. He later moved into club management with Bayern Munich and now has a role as club president.

Beckenbauer as W. Germany's manager in 1990

Beckenbauer (left) and Cruyff (right) meeting in a European Cup match in 1973 between Bayern Munich and Ajax.

SWEEPING UP
Playing behind the back markers, the sweeper casts a masterful eye over the proceedings, making crucial tackles, distributing the ball, and foraging forward. Franz Beckenbauer brought an attacking approach to the role and set the standard for all who followed.

JOHAN CRUYFF

JOHAN CRUYFF'S SKILLFUL "TURN" in the 1974 World Cup has probably been copied by more players the world over than any other technique. A graceful, dominating figure on the field, his passing ability was second to none. He led Holland to the 1974 World Cup Final and, with Dutch team Ajax, he won three European Cups in a row. He went on to play for Barcelona and after helping them to a Spanish League victory, he later became their most successful manager.

Factfile

Born: 4.25.47 Amsterdam, Holland
Clubs: Ajax 1965-73 311 appearances, 252 goals; **Barcelona** 1973-78 186 appearances, 61 goals; **Los Angeles Aztecs** 1979 27 appearances, 14 goals; **Washington Diplomats** 1980-81 32 appearances, 12 goals; **Levante** 1981 10 appearances, 2 goals; **Ajax** 1981-83 46 appearances, 16 goals; **Feyenoord** 1983-84 44 appearances, 13 goals
International Record:
Holland 1966-78
48 appearances, 33 goals

Johan Cruyff demonstrates his spectacular skills against defender, Berti Vogts, in the 1974 World Cup Final against W. Germany.

Cruyff was the first player to be voted European Soccer Player of the Year for three seasons running.

NIMBLE FEET
Cruyff became known for his astounding ball control. He would bring his foot over the ball, push it back, then twist his body around to leave the defender totally bamboozled.

SO NEAR AND YET ...
The 1974 World Cup finals tournament gave Cruyff a chance to really shine on the world stage. His brilliance helped Holland to the Final, but they were unable to defeat the host, West Germany, and Cruyff had to be content with a runner-up medal after losing 2-1.

Cruyff in his role as manager of Barcelona talking to defender Albert Ferrer, 1996

THREE IN A ROW
Dutch clubs dominated the European Cup in the early 1970s, and after Feyenoord's victory in 1970, Ajax, led by Cruyff, won for the next three years. The 1972 victory over Italian team Internazionale was particularly pleasing for Cruyff since he scored both goals in the 2-0 win.

THE BOSS
As manager of Barcelona, Cruyff led the Spanish team to their first ever European Cup victory in 1992. He also continued his tradition of consecutive victories; with him at the helm, Barcelona won the championship from 1991 to 1994. He left Barcelona in 1996.

RUUD GULLIT

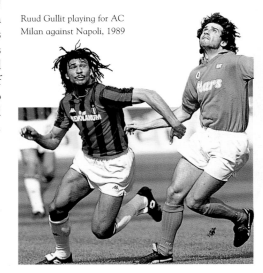

RUUD GULLIT WAS ONE of the game's most versatile players. Whether in attack, midfield, or even defense, he had a commanding presence, passing the ball with pinpoint accuracy, dribbling past defenders as if they weren't there, or powerfully heading the ball into the net. In 1988, Ruud Gullit raised the European Championship trophy to mark his nation's finest moment.

The Dutch star during the 1992 European Championship semifinal against Denmark. The final score was a 2-2 tie, but Denmark won the penalty shoot-out 5-4.

Factfile

Born: 9.1.62 Amsterdam, Holland
Clubs: **Haarlem** 1979-82
   89 appearances, 30 goals
   Feyenoord 1982-85
   85 appearances, 30 goals
   PSV Eindhoven 1985-87
   68 appearances, 46 goals
   AC Milan 1987-93
   117 appearances, 35 goals
   Sampdoria 1993-94
   31 appearances, 15 goals
   AC Milan 1994
   8 appearances, 3 goals
   Sampdoria 1994-95
   22 appearances, 9 goals
   Chelsea 1995-
   31 appearances, 3 goals
International Record:
   Holland 1981-93
   65 appearances, 16 goals

Ruud Gullit as captain of Holland in the 1988 European Championship Final. Holland beat the USSR 2-0.

THE MAGIC OF MILAN
In his time at AC Milan, Gullit won three Italian League championships and two European Cups. In 1987, his first season with the club, he was voted European and World Soccer Player of the Year, and dedicated both awards to Nelson Mandela, who was still imprisoned in South Africa at the time.

A NEW CHALLENGE
In 1995, Gullit joined top English club Chelsea, and in 1996 he took over as player-manager. In his first season as manager, Gullit led Chelsea to the 1997 English FA Cup Final, which they won against Middlesbrough 2-0.

Ruud Gullit playing for AC Milan against Napoli, 1989

Knee injuries badly affected Gullit's career at the beginning of the 1990s, but he injected new life into his game with a move to Chelsea in 1995.

The powerful Maradona could find a way through the strongest defense.

DIEGO MARADONA

UNDOUBTEDLY THE BEST player of his generation, when Diego Maradona was playing at the peak of his game, he was unstoppable. Small and powerful, his control was immaculate and he could weave his way past defenders effortlessly. He captained Argentina to World Cup victory in 1986, and in 1987 and 1990 helped Italian team Napoli win the Italian League championship. He also led Argentina to the 1990 World Cup Final, which they lost to West Germany.

Factfile

Born:	10.30.60 Buenos Aires, Argentina
Clubs:	**Argentinos Juniors** 1976-80
	116 appearances, 28 goals
	Boca Juniors 1980-82
	40 appearances, 28 goals
	Barcelona 1982-84
	36 appearances, 22 goals
	Napoli 1984-91
	186 appearances, 81 goals
	Seville 1992-93
	26 appearances, 5 goals
	Newells Old Boys 1993-94
	13 appearances, 4 goals
	Boca Juniors 1995
	24 appearances, 8 goals
International Record:	
	Argentina 1977-94
	90 appearances, 33 goals

The 1986 World Cup saw Maradona playing the finest soccer of his career. His amazingly accurate pass in the Final led to Jorge Burruchaga scoring the winner in Argentina's 3-2 victory against W. Germany.

A HELPING HAND

Maradona scored both goals in Argentina's 2-1 World Cup quarterfinal win against England in 1986. His first was regarded by many as a hand ball. The second was one of the greatest solo efforts in World Cup history.

NEAPOLITAN HEAVEN

When Maradona was transferred from Barcelona to Napoli for £5 million ($8 million) in 1984, the Italian club was expecting a big return for their money. They were not disappointed since he led them to an Italian League and Cup double in 1987, and their first ever European trophy when Napoli won the UEFA Cup in 1989.

THE BOTTOM OF THE WORLD

In 1991, Maradona was found guilty of drug abuse and given a 15-month worldwide ban. On his return, he still looked formidable, but was thrown out of the 1994 World Cup when he failed a drug test again. In 1995, Maradona returned to the game, playing with Boca Juniors in Argentina.

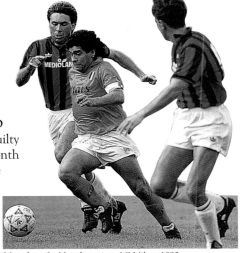

Maradona for Napoli against AC Milan, 1990

GEORGE BEST

A YEAR TO REMEMBER
In 1968, Best scored Manchester United's second goal as they defeated Benfica of Portugal 4-1 to become the first English club to win the European Cup. That year he was also named European Soccer Player of the Year.

BEING DESCRIBED BY PELE AS, "the best soccer player I have ever seen," is about as high an accolade as any soccer player could wish for. George Best was British soccer's most naturally gifted player, who was able to conjure up goals from the most unlikely of positions. He moved with grace and athleticism, and his magical ball skills and marvelous balance left defenders quaking in his wake. The lad from Northern Ireland became Britain's first "superstar" soccer player.

Factfile

Born: 5.22.46 Belfast, N. Ireland
Clubs: **Manchester United** 1963-75
361 appearances, 137 goals
Stockport County 1975-76
3 appearances, 2 goals
Los Angeles Aztecs 1976-78
61 appearances, 29 goals
Cork Celtic 1976
16 appearances, 4 goals
Fulham 1976-78
42 appearances, 8 goals
Fort Lauderdale Strikers 1978-79
33 appearances, 7 goals
Hibernian 1979-80
27 appearances, 4 goals
San Jose Earthquakes 1980-83
56 appearances, 21 goals
Bournemouth 1983-84
5 appearances, 0 goals
International Record: N. Ireland
1964-78 37 appearances, 9 goals

LIFE IN THE FAST LANE
Best led a flamboyant lifestyle, and was often seen in casinos and nightclubs. It was believed that this had an effect on his game and many feel he never truly fulfilled his potential.

George Best for N. Ireland against Peter Storey for England

SIXTH HEAVEN
On February 7, 1970, Manchester United beat Northampton Town 8-2 in an FA Cup fifth round game. Best scored six goals that day, a club record that still stands today.

THE HOLY TRINITY
Best was at his peak during the latter half of the 1960s. Together with Bobby Charlton and Denis Law up front, Best formed a strike force that propelled Manchester United to the English League title in 1965 and 1967.

Best was one of the deadliest finishers in the English League. He could also tackle as effectively as any defender, and his superb dribbling skills made him a delight to watch.

MICHEL PLATINI

Factfile

Born:	6.21.55 Joeuf, France
Clubs:	**Nancy Lorraine 1972-79**
	175 appearances, 98 goals
	St.-Etienne 1979-82
	107 appearances, 58 goals
	Juventus 1982-87
	147 appearances, 68 goals
International Record:	
	France 1976-87
	72 appearances, 41 goals

THE GREATEST PERIOD in French soccer-playing history is without a doubt the mid-1980s. With Michel Platini as captain, France won the European Championship in 1984, playing soccer that was both exhilarating and flowing. Platini was the general, leading a team packed with talent from midfield. He could pass the ball with pinpoint accuracy from one end of the field to the other and was deadly with free kicks just outside the opposition's penalty area.

Completing a hat trick against Belgium in 1984

THE AGONY ...

After battling to a 3-3 tie against West Germany in the 1982 World Cup semifinal, France and Platini suffered the pain of being the first team to go out of a World Cup in a penalty shoot-out. The Germans won the shoot-out 5-4.

Platini, the French Captain, holds the European Championship trophy.

... AND THE ECSTASY

It was a different story for Platini in 1984. With the European Championship held on their own soil, France dominated the tournament, playing some brilliant soccer. Platini was outstanding, and was on the score sheet in every game, including the Final against Spain, in which he scored the opening goal.

Platini for Juventus against Rome in Serie A of the Italian League

KING OF EUROPE

In 1982, Platini signed with Italian giant Juventus. In a glorious period, he was the Italian League's top scorer three times, was named European Soccer Player of the Year in 1983, 1984, and 1985, and scored the only goal in Juventus's first European Cup win, when they beat Liverpool 1-0 in 1985. He retired in 1987 and was manager of the French national team until 1992.

Platini scored nine goals in the 1984 European Championship – this is the highest number of goals scored by a player in any European Championship.

BOBBY CHARLTON

Bobby Charlton still holds the record for the highest number of goals scored for England.

SIR BOBBY CHARLTON is England's most famous soccer player. He was a World Cup winner in 1966 and, with Manchester United, he won three English League championships and a European Cup winners' medal. A midfielder with a ferocious shot, he scored two goals in Manchester United's 4-1 win over Benfica in the 1968 European Cup Final.

Factfile

Born: 10.11.37 Ashington, England
Clubs: **Manchester United 1954-73** 754 appearances, 247 goals
Preston North End 1974-75 38 appearances, 8 goals
International Record: **England 1958-70** 106 appearances, 49 goals

WHAT A SHOT!
Charlton had a powerful shot due to his impeccable sense of timing. His best goals – many of which thundered into the net from way outside the penalty area – are among the most spectacular ever seen in the English League.

EUSEBIO

ONE OF MANY players dubbed "the new Pele," Eusebio da Silva Ferreira probably came nearer than most to deserving it. He was a fast, skillful attacker at the heart of the Benfica team of the early 1960s. He was the top scorer in the 1966 World Cup with nine goals, and has scored more international goals than any other Portuguese player.

Factfile

Born: 1.25.42 Lourenço Marques, Mozambique
Club: **Benfica 1961-74** 365 appearances, 383 goals
International Record: **Portugal 1961-73** 64 appearances, 41 goals

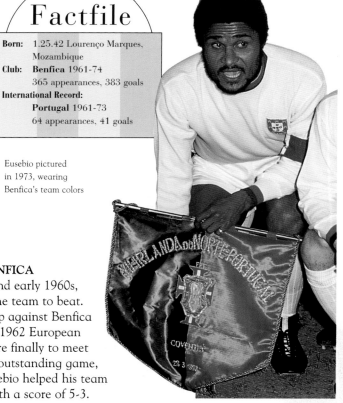

Eusebio pictured in 1973, wearing Benfica's team colors

PLAYING FOR BENFICA
In the late 1950s and early 1960s, Real Madrid was the team to beat. When they came up against Benfica and Eusebio in the 1962 European Cup Final, they were finally to meet their match. In an outstanding game, two goals from Eusebio helped his team come out on top with a score of 5-3.

FERENC PUSKAS

FERENC PUSKAS LED HUNGARY during their greatest period. Known as the "Galloping Major," due to his rank in the army, Puskas possessed a lethal left foot and tantalized defenders with his great skill and close ball control. He led Hungary to Olympic victory in 1952 and the World Cup Final in 1954, which they lost 3-2 to West Germany. His greatest success at club level came in Spain with Real Madrid, with whom he won the European Cup in 1960. He was top scorer in the Spanish League four times.

Factfile

Born: 4.2.27 Budapest, Hungary
Clubs: **Kispet**
(later named Honved)
1943-55 290 appearances, 319 goals
Real Madrid 1958-66
261 appearances, 232 goals
International Record:
Hungary 1945-56
84 appearances, 82 goals
Spain 1962
4 appearances, 0 goals

In 1960, Puskas was the first man to score four goals in a European Cup Final. Real Madrid beat Eintracht Frankfurt 7-3.

Puskas exchanges flags with the England captain in 1953.

END OF AN ERA
When Hungary played England in 1953, England had never lost at Wembley to foreign opposition. But Hungary shattered that record, beating England 6-3. Puskas scored two that day, one of which is notable for the way he dragged the ball back with the sole of his foot before swiveling and firing a left-foot shot past the England goalkeeper.

ALFREDO DI STEFANO

REAL MADRID DOMINATED European soccer in the late 1950s and early 1960s. That superiority was in no small part thanks to Alfredo Di Stefano. His clever reading of the game and immaculate sense of when to release the ball made him a force to be reckoned with. Internationally, he played for Argentina and Spain. He was once kidnapped for three days while playing for Real Madrid in Venezuela.

Factfile

Born: 7.4.26 Buenos Aires, Argentina
Clubs: **Huracan** 1944-45
45 appearances, 29 goals; **River Plate** 1946-49 66 appearances, 50 goals; **Millionarios** 1949-53 290 appearances, 260 goals; **Real Madrid** 1953-64 624 appearances, 405 goals; **Español** 1964-65 16 appearances, 4 goals
International Record:
Argentina 1947-48
8 appearances, 5 goals
Spain 1957-61
31 appearances, 21 goals

FIVE GREAT FINALS
Real Madrid won the first five European Cups between 1956 and 1960. Di Stefano scored in every Final, including a hat trick in their legendary 7-3 victory over Eintracht Frankfurt in 1960.

Di Stefano ties for Real Madrid in the 1960 European Cup Final against Eintracht Frankfurt at Hampden Park, Glasgow.

KENNY DALGLISH

PROBABLY THE GREATEST Scottish player ever, Dalglish had incredible skill and determination and could turn defenders inside out. His achievements as a player and a manager are unmatched in British soccer. He became player-manager of Liverpool in 1985 and managed Blackburn Rovers to the English League championship in 1995. He is now managing Newcastle United.

Factfile

Born:	3.4.51 Glasgow, Scotland
Clubs:	**Celtic** 1967-77
	204 appearances, 112 goals
	Liverpool 1977-90
	354 appearances, 118 goals
International Record:	
	Scotland 1972-87
	102 appearances, 30 goals

Dalglish for Liverpool with Trevor Peake of Coventry

A WEE SCOTTISH LAD
Dalglish made his debut for Celtic at the age of 17. By the time he left to go to Liverpool in 1977, he had won four Scottish League and four Scottish Cup winners' medals. His hallmarks were excellent, close ball control and an ability to shield the ball from defenders. He also had a keen eye for a defense-splitting pass.

ROGER MILLA

THE FIRST MAN to be named African Soccer Player of the Year twice, first in 1976 and then again in 1990, Cameroon's Roger Milla really came to the attention of the world's soccer-playing elite during the 1990 World Cup. Cameroon's progression to the quarterfinals put African soccer on the map. In Roger Milla they had a hugely talented showman, who liked nothing more than to entertain the crowds with his great skill and goalscoring abilities.

Milla is both the oldest player to appear and the oldest to score a goal in a World Cup finals tournament. The latter came against Russia in the 1994 World Cup. He was then 42 years of age.

Factfile

Born:	5.20.52 Cameroon
Clubs:	**Leopard Douala** 1968-73
	Tonnerre Yaounde 1973-77
	Valenciennes 1977-79
	Monaco 1979-80
	Bastia 1980-84
	St.-Etienne 1984-86
	Montpellier 1986-88
	Toulouse 1988-89
	St.-Pierroise 1989
	(Retired 1989-90)
	Puebla 1991
International Record:	
	Cameroon 1972-94
	Complete records for goals and appearances not available.

GOAL CELEBRATION
Roger Milla can lay claim to having started the trend of unusual goal celebrations. After each of his four goals in the 1990 World Cup he ran to the corner flag and wiggled around it.

KARL-HEINZ RUMMENIGGE

ARGUABLY WEST GERMANY'S most important player in the late 1970s and early 1980s, Rummenigge was hugely influential during his country's World Cup campaigns of 1978, 1982, and 1986. Named European Soccer Player of the Year twice, he has won European Cup and World Club Championship winners' medals.

OUTSTANDING SCORER
Rummenigge scored five goals in the 1982 World Cup and was on the score sheet when West Germany were beaten 3-2 by Argentina in the Final of the 1986 tournament.

Factfile
Born:	9.25.55 Lippstadt, W. Germany
Clubs:	**Bayern Munich** 1974-84
	300 appearances, 162 goals
	Internazionale 1984-87
	64 appearances, 24 goals
	Servette 1987-89
	50 appearances, 34 goals
International Record:	
	West Germany 1976-86
	95 appearances, 45 goals

Rummenigge leaves another defender flailing in his wake.

TWO GREAT VICTORIES
In 1976, Rummenigge was on the Bayern Munich team that defeated Saint-Etienne 1-0 to win the European Cup. Later that year, he helped the club to a cumulative 2-0 victory over two rounds against Brazilian team Cruzeiro, to win the World Club Cup.

LEV YASHIN

INVARIABLY CLAD ALL IN BLACK, the Russian goalkeeper Lev Yashin had a dogged determination and competitive spirit that was second to none. Coupled with incredible reflexes and agility, he possessed great anticipation and was a brilliant shot-stopper. He was his country's goalkeeper for twenty years and, with his club Dynamo Moscow, he won four Soviet League championships.

Factfile
Born:	10.22.29 Moscow, Russia
Club:	**Dynamo Moscow** 1951-70
	326 appearances
International Record:	
	Soviet Union 1954-70
	78 appearances

UNIQUE AWARDS
In 1963, Yashin was named European Soccer Player of the Year and he remains to this day the only goalkeeper to have been given that honor. He is also the only soccer player to have been awarded the Soviet Union's Order of Lenin, which he received in 1969.

AN EXCEPTIONAL PERFORMANCE
Yashin played superbly throughout the first European Championship tournament in 1960, and was in excellent form during the 2-1 final victory against Yugoslavia.

Another dynamic save by Yashin (left), limiting the Soviet defeat at the hands of W. Germany in the 1966 World Cup semifinals. The final score was 2-1.

Punching away a corner in the 1958 World Cup during a 2-2 tie with England

GORDON BANKS

Factfile

Born:	12.20.37 Sheffield, England
Clubs:	**Chesterfield** 1955-59
	23 appearances
	Leicester City 1959-67
	293 appearances
	Stoke City 1967-72
	194 appearances
International Record:	
	England 1963-72
	73 appearances

BANKS WAS HAILED as the greatest keeper in the world between 1966 and 1970. His amazing athleticism allowed him to pull off saves that others would have no hope of accomplishing. As the last line of defense, he was inspirational. Sadly, he had to quit in 1972 after losing an eye in a car accident.

Banks saves the ball (left) in the 1966 World Cup Final against W. Germany, which England won 4-2.

Banks makes his famous save, clearing Pele's header in the 1970 World Cup.

THE WORLD'S GREATEST SAVE
When Pele headed Jairzinho's cross toward the net during the 1970 World Cup clash between England and Brazil, it looked like a certain goal. Banks raced across and dived, but appeared to be beaten by the ball's bounce. Incredibly, he managed to twist upward in midair and deflect the ball over the crossbar.

DINO ZOFF

Zoff leaps to make a save, securing Italy's 3-1 victory over W. Germany in the 1982 World Cup Final.

Factfile

Born:	2.28.42 Mariano del Briuli, Italy
Clubs:	**Udinese** 1961-63
	4 appearances
	Mantova 1963-67
	93 appearances
	Napoli 1967-72
	143 appearances
	Juventus 1972-83
	330 appearances
International Record:	
	Italy 1968-82
	112 appearances

ITALIAN DEFENSES HAVE always been notoriously hard to break down, but when Dino Zoff was in the goal, that task was made much harder. A tall, commanding figure, he had a steely resolve that made him almost impossible to beat. His proudest moment was captaining Italy to World Cup triumph in 1982. As a player with club team Juventus, he won six Italian League titles and the UEFA Cup.

A CLEAN SLATE
Between September 1973 and June 1974, Zoff did not concede a goal at international level for an incredible 1,143 minutes. The run extended over twelve matches and was only broken when Haiti scored against Italy in the World Cup.

Zoff was the first Italian to make 100 international appearances.

The winning goal from the 1986 World Cup Final

THE FIFA WORLD CUP

It is the dream of every soccer player to win the World Cup. Those

who have done so can rightly call themselves the best in the world.

Held every four years, the World Cup has been a showcase

for some of the greatest soccer ever seen, played by some

of the greatest players ever known.

A DREAM BEGINS

French sculptor, Albert Lafleur, designed the World Cup trophy, which became known as the Jules Rimet trophy.

IN THE EARLY 1900S, the amateur Olympic soccer tournament was considered by many to be the world's premier international soccer competition. However, as teams became increasingly professional, there was a need for a new tournament. In 1928, Jules Rimet, the then-president of FIFA and the French Football Association, put forward a motion that there should be a World Cup competition open to every nation and held every four years. The motion was passed and the following year Olympic-champion Uruguay hosted the first World Cup.

Jules Rimet presents the World Cup trophy to the President of the Uruguayan Football Association at the start of the first tournament.

1930 URUGUAY

Argentina's Pecucelle scores to tie in the Final, but Uruguay went on to win 4-2.

THE FINALISTS	
Argentina	Paraguay
Belgium	Peru
Bolivia	Romania
Brazil	Uruguay
Chile	US
France	Yugoslavia
Mexico	

THE TOURNAMENT
The 13 teams were split into four groups, and the winners of each group progressed to the semifinals. Both semifinals ended with 6-1 scores. Argentina beat the US, and Uruguay beat Yugoslavia.

Uruguay in action

ALTHOUGH THE host nation offered to pay everyone's travel expenses, only four European teams, France, Belgium, Yugoslavia, and Romania, made the long boat trip to Uruguay. They were joined by eight teams from South and Central America, plus the US, and on July 13, 1930 the first World Cup competition kicked off with France against Mexico (France won 4-1).

Argentina's goalkeeper, Botasso, is unable to stop Dorado's shot. It was Uruguay's first goal in the Final.

THE FINAL:
Uruguay 4; Argentina 2
With Uruguay as Olympic champions and Argentina as South American champions, there couldn't have been two more apt opponents for the first World Cup Final. The match was very much a game of two halves. Uruguay scored in the 12th minute, but Argentina tied then scored again to lead at halftime. The second half, however, belonged to Uruguay. They scored three times to win 4-2 and become the first world champions.

1934 ITALY

THE SECOND WORLD CUP was the first in which teams went through a qualifying tournament. Out of the 31 teams entering the qualifying round, 16 got through to the finals tournament, which kicked off on May 27. Holders Uruguay did not enter.

Italy's Allemandi against the US keeper

THE TOURNAMENT
In the finals tournament the 16 teams were drawn against each other in a straightforward knockout competition. Italy, who had cruised past the US 7-1 in the first round, needed a rematch to beat Spain 1-0 in the next, then beat Austria 1-0 to reach the Final. Czechoslovakia beat Germany 3-1 in the other semifinal.

THE FINALISTS	
Argentina	Hungary
Austria	Italy
Belgium	Romania
Brazil	Spain
Czech.	Sweden
Egypt	Switzerland
France	US
Germany	
Holland	

Schiavio's spectacular volley for Italy, watched by teammates Meazza and Orsi

THE FINAL:
Italy 2; Czechoslovakia 1
(After overtime)
In front of 55,000 people, it was the Czechs who scored first in the 70th minute. They could have sealed victory, but missed two good chances. Then, with the crowd desperate for a home victory, Italy tied in the 82nd minute. In overtime it was the Italians who managed to summon up more energy and, when Schiavio scored after 95 minutes, they held on to win.

Manager Vittorio Pozzo carried by his victorious team

1938 FRANCE

FRANCE WAS CHOSEN to host the 1938 World Cup ahead of Argentina, a decision which meant that this tournament became the least representative ever. Only three non-European teams were involved and two of those, Cuba and the Dutch East Indies, were there because of byes in the qualifying stages.

Peracio heads Brazil's fourth goal past Poland's goalkeeper Madejski.

THE FINALISTS	
Belgium	Hungary
Brazil	Italy
Cuba	Norway
Czech.	Poland
Dutch E. Indies	Romania
France	Sweden
Germany	Switzerland
Holland	

THE TOURNAMENT
The 1934 format was retained. The outstanding match of the first round saw Brazil defeat Poland 6-5, while Cuba provided a shock by beating Romania 2-1. In the semifinals Hungary beat Sweden 5-1 and Italy beat Brazil 2-1.

The winning Italian team

Italy celebrates after becoming world champions for the second time.

THE FINAL:
Italy 4; Hungary 2
Hungary had high hopes of defeating World Cup holders Italy, but Italy's speed and goalscoring ability saw them race to a 3-1 lead by halftime. Sarosi scored for Hungary in the 70th minute, but 12 minutes later, Italy's star Piola made it 4-2 to give Italy the second win they had hoped for.

 Top goalscorers 1934: Nejedly 4 (Czechoslovakia); Schiavio 4 (Italy); Conen 4 (Germany). 1938: Leonidas 8 (Brazil); Szengeller 7 (Hungary); Piola 5 (Italy).

Above, Obdulio Varela, captain of the Uruguay team.
Below, the US defeated England 1-0 in this first round match.

1950 BRAZIL

THE SECOND WORLD WAR put a stop to the World Cup for 12 years, but in South America soccer was barely affected so Brazil was chosen to host the 1950 tournament. Again, the qualifying competition was a little disorganized and a number of teams dropped out. Among the final 13, England made a first appearance, and Uruguay returned for the first time since winning in 1930.

The opening ceremony was a lavish affair at the newly built Maracana Stadium.

THE FINALISTS	
Bolivia	Spain
Brazil	Sweden
Chile	Switzerland
England	Uruguay
Italy	US
Mexico	Yugoslavia
Paraguay	

Brazil against Mexico in a first round match that they won 4-0. Playing in front of home crowds, Brazil had high hopes of reaching the Final.

THE FIRST ROUND GROUPS

The teams were split into four groups. Group Four consisted of only Uruguay and Bolivia due to the last-minute withdrawal of France after they decided that they didn't want to make the journey to Brazil. England's debut was notable only because they suffered one of the most surprising upsets in international soccer by losing 1-0 to the US in the first round.

THE ROUTE TO THE FINAL

The four group winners, Brazil, Uruguay, Sweden, and Spain, went into a final group where each team played each other. Brazil beat Sweden and Spain, 7-1 and 6-1 respectively. Uruguay defeated Sweden and tied with Spain, so the last group match between the two South American giants was to be decisive.

THE FINAL:
Uruguay 2; Brazil 1

Due to the final round being a group competition, Brazil only needed a tie against Uruguay to win the tournament. On July 16 a crowd made up almost entirely of Brazilians was not even considering anything less. When Friaca scored for Brazil two minutes into the second half, everything seemed to be going to plan. Then, after 66 minutes, Uruguay's Schiaffino tied. Incredibly, 11 minutes from the final whistle another goal, this time from Ghiggia, put Uruguay in the lead. They held on until the end of the match to become champions and thousands of Brazilians went home very disappointed.

Amid a goalmouth scramble, the referee signals the end of the Final.

  Top goalscorers: Ademir 9 (Brazil); Schiaffino 6 (Uruguay); Zarra 5 (Spain).

1954 SWITZERLAND

In 1946, FIFA HAD DECIDED that Switzerland should host the 1954 tournament. Switzerland was the only European contender at the time and since 1954 was also the 50th anniversary of FIFA, whose headquarters are in Zurich, Switzerland was the ideal choice. The qualifying tournament was more representative than it had been four years before, and Scotland, South Korea, and Turkey got through to the finals tournament for the first time.

Morlock breaks through Hungary's defense to score W. Germany's first goal in the Final.

THE FORMAT

The 16 teams were split into four groups. Rather oddly though, each group had two seeded teams who only played two games against the unseeded teams. The top two of each group went on to a knockout phase.

Hungary defeated Brazil 4-2 in this quarterfinal, which ended in a riot. Swiss police rushed onto the field to separate the fighting players. The match became known as the "Battle of Berne." Here, Humberto of Brazil is held back as police lead off Brazil's assistant coach.

Kocsis (right) helps Hungary defeat Brazil 4-2.

THE ROUTE TO THE FINAL

Hungary was the strong favorite and, after thrashing South Korea 9-0 and West Germany 8-3 they seemed unstoppable. They advanced to the Final by defeating Brazil and Uruguay. There they met West Germany for the second time in the tournament. West Germany had beaten Yugoslavia and Austria in the knockout phase.

THE FINAL:
West Germany 3; Hungary 2

After their 8-3 victory over West Germany earlier in the competition, the Hungarians were confident and two goals in the first eight minutes seemed to put them on the right course. However, the Germans hit back with two goals of their own in the next eight minutes, making the score 2-2 with under a quarter of the match played. For the next 65 minutes, with the rain lashing down, Hungary besieged the German goal, but amazingly, they failed to score.

LAST MINUTES

Overtime seemed inevitable until, five minutes from the end, West Germany scored to seal their victory.

Jules Rimet, president of FIFA, at the 1954 Final

Kocsis of Hungary was the top goalscorer of the 1954 finals tournament. He scored four of Hungary's eight goals against W. Germany in the first round, and 11 in the tournament as a whole.

THE FINALISTS

Austria	Mexico
Scotland	Belgium
Brazil	S. Korea
Switzerland	Czech.
England	Turkey
France	Uruguay
Hungary	W. Germany
Italy	Yugoslavia

1958 SWEDEN

THE COMPETITION STAYED in Europe in 1958, rather than returning to South America, and was the most representative yet, even though less than half of FIFA's membership entered. Argentina made a welcome return to the tournament and all four of the United Kingdom's countries qualified. Italy and Uruguay, who between them had won four of the first five championships, were both absent having failed to qualify.

THE TOURNAMENT

The 16 finalists were split into four groups and this time all the teams played each other. The top two of each group progressed to a knockout phase. Sweden topped their group and defeated the Soviet Union and West Germany to get to the Final. The other team to progress was Brazil, who beat France 5-2 in their semifinal.

Vava scores Brazil's fourth goal against France in their semifinal.

THE FINAL

Brazil 5; Sweden 2

A heavily rain-sodden field was expected to favor home team Sweden and when they took the lead after only four minutes, Brazil might have collapsed. However, thanks to two goals by Vava, at halftime Brazil were leading 2-1. The second half belonged to the young Pelé. In a dazzling display, he scored Brazil's third goal, then Zagalo made it 4-1. Sweden did pull a goal back, but Pelé scored again in the 89th minute. It was the first time a team had won the World Cup outside of their own continent, and the first time the world had witnessed the brilliance of Pelé.

A 17-year-old Pelé sheds tears of joy with Djalma Santos, Didi, and Gilmar after Brazil's win in the Final.

Above, Pelé heads the ball and below, he shoots against Sweden's goalkeeper, Kalle Svensson.

Brazil beating the Soviet Union 2-0 in the first round

THE FINALISTS		
N. Ireland	Argentina	
Paraguay	Austria	
Scotland	Brazil	
Soviet Union	Czech.	
Sweden	England	
W. Germany	France	
Wales	Hungary	
Yugoslavia	Mexico	

Above, Lev Yashin for the Soviet Union fails to stop Derek Kevan's shot from crossing the line. It was the first goal for England in this match. The game ended 2-2.

1962 CHILE

CHILE WAS CHOSEN to host the 1962 World Cup largely due to the efforts of the president of the Chilean FA, Carlos Dittborn. After a massive earthquake in 1960, he summed up Chile's desperation to hold the tournament when he said, "We have nothing. That is why we must have the World Cup." Sadly, Dittborn died a month before the finals tournament. Once again, the qualifying teams were entirely from Europe and South and Central America since the teams from Africa and Asia were defeated in the qualifying rounds.

Zito scores Brazil's second goal from a header in the 69th minute.

Mauro holds the Jules Rimet trophy aloft for Brazil after they retain their title as world champions.

THE TOURNAMENT

The format of the competition remained the same as in 1958. Brazil and Czechoslovakia both qualified from the same group and made it to the semifinals.

Brazil beat Chile 4-2 and Czechoslovakia beat Yugoslavia 3-1. Pele's tournament finished early when he was injured in the first round.

THE FINALISTS

Argentina	Italy
Brazil	Mexico
Bulgaria	Soviet Union
Chile	Spain
Colombia	Switzerland
Czech.	Uruguay
England	W. Germany
Hungary	Yugoslavia

THE FINAL:

Brazil 3; Czechoslovakia 1

Czechoslovakia was a team with a strong defense, but little attacking flair. Yet they surprised everyone by taking the lead after 16 minutes. It was short-lived however, since two minutes later Brazil tied after a mistake by the Czech goalkeeper, Schroiff. Halfway through the second half, Brazil took the lead through Amarildo, Pele's replacement. Then another goalkeeping error allowed them to score again to win 3-1. Even without Pele, Brazil had retained their title.

Czech goalkeeper Schroiff fails to stop Brazil's free kick in the Final.

Uwe Seeler for W. Germany challenges Yugoslavia's goalkeeper in a quarterfinal match. W. Germany lost the game 1-0.

Home team Chile was defeated 4-2 by Brazil in the semifinals shown above (Chile in red uniforms).

Top goalscorers: Eusebio 9 (Portugal); Haller 5 (West Germany);
Beckenbauer 4 (West Germany).

1966 ENGLAND

World Cup Willie, the official 1966 mascot

ENGLAND, SPAIN, AND WEST GERMANY all put forward bids to stage the World Cup in 1966, but in the end England was awarded the tournament.

Soccer had come home to the country that invented the game as we know it today. The number of countries entering the qualifying rounds continued to grow, with 71 teams this time. However, Africa and Asia were awarded only one place in the finals between them, so most of the teams from those continents dropped out. The eventual qualifier for that place was North Korea.

THE FINALISTS

Argentina	Mexico
Brazil	N. Korea
Bulgaria	Portugal
Chile	Soviet Union
England	Spain
France	Switzerland
Hungary	Uruguay
Italy	W. Germany

THE FIRST ROUND

The previous format was repeated. North Korea were surprise victors over Italy, and qualified for the knockout phase. Pele once again suffered injury and Brazil finished only third in their group.

Italy's players make a brave attempt to tie, but North Korea was to win this first round match 1-0 and qualify for the knockout phase.

THE ROUTE TO THE FINAL

After topping their group, England then defeated Argentina and Portugal en route to the Final. There they met West Germany who had beaten Uruguay and the Soviet Union in the knockout phase. The North Koreans didn't quite make it to the Final after throwing away a three-goal lead in their quarter-final match against Portugal.

The Soviets losing 2-1 to W. Germany in the semifinals

Eusebio in tears after England defeated Portugal 2-1 in the semifinals

England's great defender and captain, Bobby Moore

THE FINAL
England 4; West Germany 2 (After overtime)

In an even contest, Haller scored for West Germany after 13 minutes, but Hurst tied for England by halftime. After 77 minutes Peters scored and England looked set for victory until, seconds from the end, West Germany tied through Weber to take the game into overtime. Hurst then hit a shot against the crossbar that bounced down and out of the goal. The referee awarded a goal, much to the disgust of West Germany. However, in the dying seconds, Hurst scored again, making him the only player to score a hat trick in a World Cup Final, and enabling England to become world champions.

1970 MEXICO

THE CHOICE OF MEXICO as host for the 1970 World Cup finals tournament was felt by many to be a little surprising. With the intense heat and altitude, it was thought that the quality of soccer might suffer. As it turned out, soccer blossomed. Holder England was strongly favored to retain their title, but West Germany was to make up for their 1966 defeat. They knocked out England 3-2 in the quarterfinals after overtime. Israel and El Salvador qualified for the first time, as did Morocco, who became the first African nation to compete in a finals tournament.

W. Germany's Müller brings the score to 2-1 in their semifinal against Italy. Italy went on to win 4-3.

Making one of the greatest saves of all time, Gordon Banks stops Pele's shot in this first stage match between Brazil and England. Brazil went on to beat England 1-0 with a goal from Jairzinho.

Peru beating Morocco 3-0 in the first round

THE TOURNAMENT

The four-group format was retained. Brazil, with a fully fit Pele, won all three of its group games as did West Germany. Italy won its group despite scoring only one goal, but they improved in the quarterfinals beating Mexico 4-1. Italy then secured a place in the Final after an exhilarating 4-3 semifinal win against West Germany. There they met Brazil who looked unstoppable after victories over Peru and Uruguay.

THE FINALISTS	
Belgium	Mexico
Brazil	Morocco
Bulgaria	Peru
Czech.	Romania
El Salvador	Soviet Union
England	Sweden
Israel	Uruguay
Italy	W. Germany

Brazil's right-winger Jairzinho (right) scored in every game for Brazil in the 1970 finals tournament.

Pele holding the Jules Rimet trophy

THE FINAL:

Brazil 4; Italy 1

In what was probably soccer's greatest team performance, Brazil was far too strong for Italy. Pele scored their first goal after 17 minutes. A defensive error allowed Italy to tie with a goal from Boninsenga, but three brilliant second-half goals, the last of which was one of the most memorable goals ever, saw Brazil cruise to victory. As world champions for a third time, they were allowed to keep the Jules Rimet trophy.

Brazil's defender Brito clears Italy's cross in the Final.

 Top goalscorers: Müller 9 (West Germany); Jairzinho 7 (Brazil); Pele 4 (Brazil).

1974 WEST GERMANY

WEST GERMANY WAS in a good position to take on the World Cup in 1974, having hosted the Olympic Games two years previously. Terrorism had ruined the Olympics, so security for the World Cup was particularly tight. The number of Asian and African teams entering the qualifying rounds rose dramatically, although they were still fighting for only two places in the finals tournament. England failed to qualify this time, having been eliminated by Poland.

The dominating Franz Beckenbauer playing in a second round group match against Poland that W. Germany won 1-0

The new FIFA trophy was presented for the first time in 1974.

Scotland against Yugoslavia in a first round group match that ended as a 1-1 tie

Yugoslavia holding Brazil to a 0-0 tie in the opening match

The brilliant Johan Cruyff (left) at the helm of the Holland team that played their unique brand of "total football"

THE TOURNAMENT
The 16 teams were still split into four groups, but this time the eight qualifiers were split into two further groups and the top team of each went on to the Final. Holland was impressive and reached its first Final. There they met the home team, West Germany.

THE FINALISTS	
Argentina	Italy
Australia	Poland
Brazil	Scotland
Bulgaria	Sweden
Chile	Uruguay
E. Germany	W. Germany
Haiti	Yugoslavia
Holland	Zaire

Müller for W. Germany scoring the winning goal in the Final against Holland.

THE FINAL:

West Germany 2; Holland 1
In an amazing start, Cruyff burst into the German penalty area and was brought down with less than a minute played. Neeskens then scored the first penalty in a World Cup Final and Holland were leading 1-0 without a German player having touched the ball! West Germany leveled the score after 25 minutes when they, too, were awarded a penalty, scored by Paul Breitner. Just before halftime, they took the lead through the irrepressible Gerd Müller. Try as they might, the Dutch couldn't break down the German defense in the second half so the new World Cup trophy went to the host nation.

The victorious team of 1974, W. Germany. Franz Beckenbauer (captain) and Helmut Schoen (coach) hold the trophy.

Top goalscorers: Lato 7 (Poland); Neeskens 5 (Holland); Szarmach 5 (Poland).

The River Plate Stadium during the opening ceremony

1978 ARGENTINA

ARGENTINA FINALLY STAGED a World Cup in 1978. At the time there were fears that political problems and delays in the construction of some stadiums would threaten the running of the tournament, but it turned out that there were no such problems. Once again, England failed to qualify, as did Uruguay, but Brazil maintained their record of playing in every finals tournament. There were still only two places in the finals for African and Asian nations, but, with more countries from these continents entering the qualifying rounds than ever before, this was the last time there would be so few.

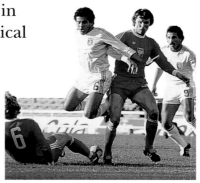

Poland beating Tunisia 1-0 in a first round match. Poland went on to win their first round group. Tunisia came in third, but was impressive beating Mexico 3-1 and tying 0-0 with W. Germany.

THE TOURNAMENT

The 1974 format was retained. Italy looked strong in the first round group games. In the second round the European challenge was taken up by Holland who, even without Cruyff, reached the Final for the second time running. Argentina, under immense pressure, secured a second round place and went on to beat Peru 6-0 to reach the Final.

THE FINALISTS	
Argentina	Mexico
Austria	Peru
Brazil	Poland
France	Scotland
Holland	Spain
Hungary	Sweden
Iran	Tunisia
Italy	W. Germany

Argentina winning 6-0 against Peru to put themselves one game away from glory

Italy made a good start to the tournament, but only managed a 0-0 tie against W. Germany in this second round match. They finished runners-up to Holland in their second round group.

THE FINAL:

Argentina 3; Holland 1 (After overtime)

A crowd of 77,000 mainly frenzied Argentinians was in no doubt of the desired outcome to the Final. Their team started well and took the lead after 37 minutes with a goal by Kempes. The Dutch battled on and were rewarded with a tying score from Nanninga after 81 minutes. But Holland couldn't muster the energy in over- time to find a winning goal. Spurred on by the home crowd, Kempes and Bertoni scored for Argentina to make them world champions for the first time.

Argentinian fans fill the air with streams of ticker tape as the Final begins.

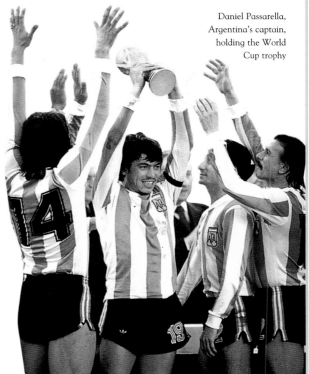

Daniel Passarella, Argentina's captain, holding the World Cup trophy

Striker Mario Kempes slots in the ball past Holland's goalkeeper, Jongbloed, to put Argentina 2-1 up in the Final.

⚽ Top goalscorers: Kempes 6 (Argentina); Rensenbrink 5 (Holland); Cubillas 5 (Peru). ⚽

1982 SPAIN

THE SPANISH ARE as fervent about soccer as the Argentineans and have some of the largest stadiums in the world. The 1982 finals tournament gave these great stadiums a chance to play host to some of the greatest soccer. The number of finalists was increased to 24. Africa and Asia were finally awarded two places each, but Europe's allocation also went up by four slots for a total of thirteen. Most of the big names were there, but once again Uruguay failed to qualify.

Lato of Poland against Scirea of Italy. Italy beat Poland 2-0 in the semifinals.

THE FINALISTS

Algeria	Hungary
Argentina	Italy
Austria	Kuwait
Belgium	N. Ireland
Brazil	New Zealand
Cameroon	Peru
Chile	Poland
Czech.	Scotland
El Salvador	Soviet Union
England	Spain
France	W. Germany
Honduras	Yugoslavia

THE EARLY ROUNDS

In the first round the 24 teams were split into six groups of four. The top two of each group qualified for the second round, where they were split into four groups of three. The winners of these groups then went on to knockout semifinals. There were some astonishing results in the first round with Hungary defeating El Salvador 10-1 and Algeria beating West Germany 2-1. Brazil looked strong but was not to get through the second round.

Hungary defeating El Salvador 10-1 in the first stage. Hungary's Kiss scored a hat trick after coming on in the 57th minute.

Paolo Rossi of Italy was the top goalscorer in the finals tournament with six goals.

Algeria beating W. Germany 2-1 in the first round. In their other two first round group matches Algeria lost 2-0 to Austria, then beat Chile 3-2.

THE ROUTE TO THE FINAL

Italy was unimpressive in the first round, but they qualified on goals scored. A 3-2 win against Brazil in the second round and a 2-0 victory over Poland in the semifinals ensured them a place in the Final. In the other semifinal, West Germany defeated France on penalties.

Marco Tardelli (who scored Italy's second goal) with the cup, and captain Dino Zoff after Italy's victory

THE FINAL:

Italy 3; West Germany 1
After an uninspiring first half, with a missed penalty by Italy, Rossi scored after 56 minutes. Italy was leading by two goals 13 minutes later, and scored a third ten minutes from the end. Breitner's strike for Germany after 82 minutes was purely a consolation goal.

Paolo Rossi celebrates after scoring Italy's first goal in the Final.

⚽ Top goalscorers 1982: Rossi 6 (Italy); Rummenigge 5 (West Germany); Zico 4 (Brazil). ⚽
1986: Lineker 6 (England); Butragueño 5 (Spain); Careca 5 (Brazil).

1986 MEXICO

Above, Butragueño for Spain against Denmark

Above, Denmark against Uruguay

COLOMBIA WAS ORIGINALLY chosen to host the 1986 World Cup, but due to economic conditions this nation had to withdraw and Mexico was chosen instead. Again, there were 24 finalists, whittled down from a record 113 initial entrants. All the major soccer-playing nations were there except Holland, and, because Mexico qualified automatically as host, the North and Central American region was represented by Canada. They had surprised everyone by making it through the qualifying rounds.

THE FINALISTS	
Algeria	Mexico
Argentina	Morocco
Belgium	N. Ireland
Brazil	Paraguay
Bulgaria	Poland
Canada	Portugal
Denmark	Scotland
England	S. Korea
France	Soviet Union
Hungary	Spain
Iraq	Uruguay
Italy	W. Germany

Maradona displays his skill as he takes the ball through the England defense. Argentina won this quarterfinal 2-1.

THE EARLY ROUNDS

As in 1982, the 24 teams were split into six groups. However, this time the top two of each group and the four best third-placed teams went through to a second round, where the tournament became a knockout competition. Denmark and Morocco were the unexpected strong outsiders of the first round. Each won their group, but neither could make it past the second round.

England's Gary Lineker (left) was the top goalscorer in this tournament with six goals.

THE ROUTE TO THE FINAL

Of the quarterfinals, three were decided on penalties and the fourth saw Maradona score twice – once, with the controversial "hand of God" – to lead his side into the semifinals. There they defeated Belgium to face a Final with West Germany who had once again beaten France in their semifinal.

THE FINAL:
Argentina 3; West Germany 2

This was a Final that swung one way and then another. Argentina took the lead midway through the first half. They produced another goal just after halftime and seemed on course for a comfortable win, but 17 minutes from the end West Germany scored, and nine minutes later they tied. Overtime looked likely, but two minutes later Maradona's superb pass found Burruchaga, who scored to give Argentina their second World Cup in eight years.

1990 ITALY

Andy Townsend (left) for the Republic of Ireland and Iosif Rotariu (right) for Romania in a second round match. Ireland won 5-4 on penalties.

Hector Marchena for Costa Rica in a second round match against Czechoslovakia. Czechoslovakia won 4-0.

ITALY HOSTED THE WORLD CUP for a second time in 1990. With two new stadiums promised and ten to refurbish, time and money were tight, but everything was ready by the start. The number of teams entering the qualifying competition went down for the first time since 1950, but there were debut appearances in the finals tournament for the Republic of Ireland, Costa Rica, and the United Arab Emirates.

Cameroon players battling against Maradona of Argentina in the first match of the tournament. Surprisingly, Cameroon won 1-0.

THE FINALISTS

Argentina	Rep. of Ireland
Austria	Romania
Belgium	Scotland
Brazil	S. Korea
Cameroon	Soviet Union
Colombia	Spain
Costa Rica	Sweden
Czech.	UAE
Egypt	Uruguay
England	US
Holland	W. Germany
Italy	Yugoslavia

THE EARLY ROUNDS
The previous format was retained and the tournament had a sensational start when Cameroon defeated holders Argentina. Cameroon topped their group and made it to the quarterfinals, where they were knocked out 3-2 by England.

Argentina and Italy in their semifinal. They tied 1-1, then Argentina won 4-3 on penalties after overtime.

THE ROUTE TO THE FINAL
Argentina qualified for the second round as one of the best third-placed teams. In the knockout stages, victories over Brazil, Yugoslavia, and Italy, the latter two on penalties, secured them a place in the Final. Their opponent was West Germany again, who had won a titanic semifinal battle against England, also on penalties.

Andreas Brehme scores the penalty for W. Germany.

THE FINAL:
West Germany 1; Argentina 0
In a competition dominated by penalty shoot-outs, it was fitting that this Final was decided by a penalty. After 85 minutes the game was goalless and seemed to be heading for overtime when West Germany's striker Völler was brought down in the Argentinian penalty area. Brehme converted the spot kick and West Germany took the title making up for their defeat in 1986. Sadly, this World Cup Final was also the first in which players were thrown out. Argentina's Monzon got the red card after 68 minutes and his teammate Dezotti was thrown out three minutes from the end.

Matthäus (left) and Völler (right) celebrate W. Germany's victory.

Pedro Monzon was the first of the two Argentinians to be thrown out in the Final.

The amazing closing ceremony
of the 1994 World Cup

1994 US

FIFA MADE FOUR important changes that were intended to make the games more exciting in the 1994 World Cup. There were measures to prevent tackling from behind, the offside rule was made more lenient, injured players were to leave the field at once to receive medical treatment, and three points, rather than two, were to be awarded for a win in the group round. Qualifiers for the finals tournament included Cameroon, South Korea, and newcomers Nigeria and Saudi Arabia as the representatives of Africa and Asia. Surprisingly, no countries from the United Kingdom qualified.

THE FINALISTS

Argentina	Morocco
Belgium	Nigeria
Bolivia	Norway
Brazil	Rep. of Ireland
Bulgaria	Romania
Cameroon	Russia
Colombia	Saudi Arabia
Germany	S. Korea
Greece	Spain
Holland	Sweden
Italy	Switzerland
Mexico	US

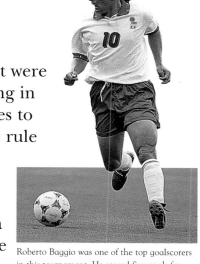

Roberto Baggio was one of the top goalscorers in this tournament. He scored five goals for Italy, including two in their semifinal.

THE TOURNAMENT

Helped by FIFA's rule changes, this tournament was full of attacking flair. The format remained the same and in the first round Nigeria topped its group, but was then narrowly defeated by Italy in the second round. Italy went on to reach the Final after defeating Spain and Bulgaria. The latter team had sensationally knocked out Germany in the quarterfinals. Brazil beat the US, Holland, then Sweden to secure their place in the Final.

Romario in a second round match that Brazil won 1-0 against the US. Brazil was playing soccer reminiscent of the great 1970 team.

Newcomer Saudi Arabia (in the white uniforms) did well beating Morocco and Belgium in the first round. They were defeated by Sweden in the second round.

Roberto Mussi of Italy (left) and Hristo Stoichkov of Bulgaria (right) in their semifinal. Italy won 2-1.

Italy's Roberto Baggio misses the penalty and Brazil wins the 1994 World Cup.

THE FINAL:

Brazil 0; Italy 0 (After overtime)

Brazil won 3-2 on penalties

Sadly, this wasn't to be a repeat of the 1970 Final. Try as they might, Brazil couldn't get past the Italians and after 120 grueling minutes the championship was decided by a penalty shoot-out. After both teams had taken four penalties the score was 3-2 to Brazil. Italy's Roberto Baggio then had to score to save his side. Unfortunately for him, he blasted the ball over the bar, which was the cue for the partying in Brazil to begin.

⚽ Top goalscorers: Salenko 6 (Russia); Stoichkov 6 (Bulgaria); Andersson 5 (Sweden); ⚽
Baggio 5 (Italy); Romario 5 (Brazil); Klinsman 5 (Germany).

The official logo for the 1998 World Cup finals tournament

THE TEN VENUES
Paris
Parc des Princes Stadium
Saint-Denis
Stade de France
Nantes
La Beaujoire Stadium
Lens
Félix Bollaert Stadium
Bordeaux
Parc Lescure Stadium
Toulouse
Municipal Stadium
Saint-Etienne
Geoffroy-Guichard Stadium
Lyon
Gerland Stadium
Montpellier
La Mosson Stadium
Marseille
Velodrome Stadium

1998 FRANCE

WITH THIRTY TWO TEAMS participating, the 1998 World Cup finals will be the biggest ever. Europe will have fourteen places, South America will have four, North and Central America will have three, while Africa has been allocated five places. Asia will have three definite finalists and the possibility of one more, since the fourth-placed Asian team will play the winners of the Oceania section for that last place. Holders Brazil and host nation France qualify automatically. The games will take place at ten venues throughout France. For the first round of the finals, the thirty two teams will be divided into eight groups of four and the four teams in each group will play each other. The top two of each group will then progress to the next round, where the competition will continue on a knockout basis.

Created especially for the championship, the little roosters are the official mascots for the 1998 World Cup.

As winners of the 1994 tournament, Brazil is among the teams favored to win the 1998 World Cup.

Playing in front of home crowds, France may have an advantage.

More than two million fans are expected to attend the 1998 World Cup, with 37 billion people watching it on television.

Whose hands will raise the trophy in 1998?

PREDICTIONS
Many would agree that the three favorite teams to win the 1998 World Cup are France, Brazil, and Germany. Argentina and Italy are also widely considered to be strong contenders. But, with more teams than ever competing in the tournament, there may be a completely new name on the World Cup trophy come July 12, 1998. Whatever happens, fans all around the globe are in for some sensational soccer.

Based on their previous World Cup performances and their European Championship win in 1996, Germany's chances are good.

WORLD CUP TRIVIA

FROM BIZARRE EVENTS TO RECORD-BREAKING MOMENTS, the World Cup has produced many memorable incidents over the years. Here are some of the most notable.

1930

• Romania played Peru in front of 300 people – the smallest crowd to attend a match in a World Cup finals tournament.
• Guillermo Stabile scored the first ever hat trick in a World Cup finals in Argentina's 6-3 win against Mexico.

1934

• Both Italy and Czechoslovakia were captained by their goalkeepers in the Final.
• Uruguay did not defend their 1930 World Cup title. Upset by Europe's reluctance to participate in 1930 and with players on strike at home, they didn't enter.

1938

• Austria's team qualified, but by the time of the finals Austria was no longer a separate country and had to withdraw.
• In the second round match between Brazil and Czechoslovakia five players were injured and three were thrown out.

1950

• India refused to take part after they were told by FIFA that players would have to wear shoes in the finals tournament.
• Brazil were so confident of winning the Final against Uruguay that they had a victory song written before the game.

1954

• Austria beat Switzerland 7-5 in the quarterfinals. This match stands as the highest scoring in a World Cup finals tournament.
• Uruguay's 4-2 defeat by Hungary in the semifinals was their first in a World Cup finals.
• Fritz and Ottmar Walter were the first brothers to win World Cup medals when Germany beat Hungary 3-2 in the Final.

1958

• For the first time, the finals were fully covered by television.
• Just Fontaine expected to be a reserve player for France. He only got a first team place due to an injury to striker Rene Biliard and went on to score 13 goals in the finals tournament.

1962

• The match between Italy and Chile became known as the "Battle of Santiago" after two Italian players were thrown out.
• Masek's goal for Czechoslovakia after 15 seconds of their match against Mexico is the fastest ever scored in a World Cup finals.

1966

• The Mexican goalkeeper Antonio Carbajal played in a fifth World Cup finals tournament – a record number of World Cup appearances.
• The host nation won the World Cup trophy for the first time in 32 years.

1970

• Red and yellow cards were used for the first time.
• In a first round match between Mexico and El Salvador, Mexico scored after taking a free kick that the referee had in fact awarded to El Salvador. The goal was allowed.

1974

• Scotland tied all three of their games in their first round group, but did not qualify for the next round. However, they ended up the only team not to lose a game in the finals tournament.
• Chile's Carlos Caszely became the first player to receive a red card in a World Cup finals in a match against West Germany.

1978

• Dutch player Rene Van der Kerkhof played in the Final with a plaster cast on his arm.
• Commercials on Argentinian TV urged people to be on their best behavior during the finals tournament.

1982

• Hungary's Laszlo Kiss scored the fastest ever hat trick in a World Cup finals tournament when he took just nine minutes to score his three goals against El Salvador in a first round match.

1986

• The Final saw West Germany play in green uniforms for the only time in their six Final appearances.
• Argentina's manager, Carlos Bilardo, was also a qualified doctor at the time of the World Cup.

1990

• Argentina's Diego Maradona won the unfortunate title of most-fouled player in this World Cup finals tournament after he was on the receiving end of no less than 53 unfair challenges.

1994

• The Pontiac Silverdrome near Detroit staged the first indoor matches at a World Cup finals tournament.
• Bulgaria, who had never won a match in a finals before this one, got to the semifinals.
• FIFA's new rule changes helped to produce a record 235 bookings.

US Soccer National History and Victory

NATIONAL PROFESSIONAL SOCCER LEAGUE (NPSL)

(Indoor) Standings through 1995

AMERICAN DIVISION	W	L	Pct	GB
(d) Cleveland Crunch	30	10	.750	–
(p) Harrison Heat	23	17	.575	7
(p) Baltimore Spirit	23	17	.575	7
(p) Buffalo Blizzard	20	20	.500	10
Dayton Dynamo	15	25	.375	15
Canton Invaders	6	34	.150	24

AMERICAN DIVISION	W	L	Pct	GB
(d) St. Louis Ambush	30	10	.750	–
(p) Kansas City Attack	29	11	.725	1
(d) Milwaukee Wave	23	17	.575	7
(p) Detroit Rockets	18	22	.450	12
Wichita Wings	17	23	.425	13
Chicago Power	6	34	.150	24

(d) earned division championship (p) earned playoff berth

CHAMPIONSHIP (BEST-OF-FIVE)
St. Louis vs. Harrisburg
(St. Louis wins championship, 4 games to 0)

April 20 – St. Louis 19, Harrisburg 9
April 22 – St. Louis 18, Harrisburg 8
April 23 – St. Louis 12, Harrisburg 7
April 25 – St. Louis 14, Harrisburg 11

US PRO LEAGUES (outdoor)

NATIONAL PROFESSIONAL SOCCER LEAGUE (1967)
During its brief existence, the NPSL recruited individual players to make up the rosters of its 10 teams. The league lasted for just a season, with the Oakland Clippers beating the Baltimore Bays by 1 goal to claim the league championship.

UNITED SOCCER ASSOCIATION (1967)
USA adopted this name, a switch from its original title – North American Soccer League – at the direction of FIFA, the international soccer federation. FIFA mandated the name change because NASL was easily confused with NPSL (National Professional Soccer League). The USA imported 12 European teams and reassigned them American names and regions. Like the NPSL, USA was short-lived. At the end of the league's one and only season, the Los Angeles Wolves (actually Wolverhampton of England) became the USA champions; they defeated the Washington Whips (actually Aberdeen of Scotland).

NORTH AMERICAN SOCCER LEAGUE (1968-1984)

The NASL was established in 1967 by a merger of the NPSL and USA, with its first competition season taking place in 1968.

NORTH AMERICAN SOCCER LEAGUE CHAMPIONS

1968 – Atlanta Chiefs
1969 – Kansas City Stars
1970 – Rochester Lancers
1971 – Dallas Tornado
1972 – New York Cosmos
1973 – Philadelphia Atoms
1974 – Los Angeles Aztecs
1975 – Tampa Bay Rowdies
1976 – Toronto Metro – Croatia
1977 – New York Cosmos
1978 – New York Cosmos
1979 – Vancouver Whitecaps
1980 – New York Cosmos
1981 – Chicago Sting
1982 – New York Cosmos
1983 – Tulsa Roughnecks
1984 – Chicago Sting

KEY DATES IN US SOCCER

1967
James P. McGuire was elected president of the newly formed North American Soccer League.

1968
On September 28, the Atlanta Chiefs beat the San Diego Toros in the first North American Soccer League (NASL) championship.

1970
The North American Soccer League split into two divisions.

1971
New York City and Toronto franchises were added for the 1971 NASL season.

1975
Soccer sensation Pele (born Edson Arantes do Nascimento) announced his intention to come out of retirement to play for the New York Cosmos. His reported three-year, $7,000,000 contract clinched his status as the highest-paid team athlete in the world.

1977
Pele's presence on an American professional helped make soccer the fastest-growing team sport in the US. In August of 1977, a new US Soccer attendance record of 77,961 spectators was achieved in East Rutherford, NJ at a playoff game between the New York Cosmos and the Fort Lauderdale Strikers.

1985
Due to financial trouble, the North American Soccer League went out of business.

1991
The US defeated Norway in the first world championship of women's soccer, held in Guangzhou, China.

1996
US Women's Soccer wins Olympic gold. Major League Soccer created.

TEST YOUR KNOWLEDGE

Answers on page 96

1. Which team shares its name with a mythological Greek hero?

2. When Barcelona won the Spanish League in 1985, who was their manager?

3. Why does the AC Milan team use the anglicized "Milan" rather than the Italian "Milano"?

4. Who was the manager of Scottish club Glasgow Celtic when they won the European Cup in 1967?

5. What was the Manchester United team originally known as?

6. How old was Stanley Matthews when he played his last game for English club Stoke City in 1965?

7. While playing in Sweden, how many goals did Michelle Akers score in 1992 to make her the top scorer in any of Sweden's professional leagues?

8. Which two brothers played for England in the 1966 World Cup Final against West Germany?

9. While playing Northern Ireland in 1952, which injured Frenchman returned to the field without realizing he'd been substituted? When did France realize that they were playing with 12 men?

10. Pele and a host of other soccer stars appeared in a movie in 1981. What was the movie's title?

11. When was Holland's biggest win and what was the score?

12. What cut short Ferenc Puskas' soccer-playing career in Hungary and how did he come to be signed for Real Madrid in 1958?

13. Just Fontaine scored a record 13 goals for France in the 1958 World Cup finals tournament in Sweden, but in which country was he born?

14. What was the nickname of Spanish striker Emilio Butragueño?

15. Which famous Swiss club has the same name as a jumping insect?

16. Who was the first player to score in three consecutive European Championships?

17. What was the average age of Nigeria's Olympic winning team of 1996?

18. When was Spain's biggest ever victory, who was it against, and what was the score?

19. A record low of 13 people turned up to an English League match in 1921 between which two teams?

20. What is the nickname of English club team Arsenal?

21. Which team was originally called the Central Uruguayan Railway Cricket Club?

22. In which city was the first ever European Cup Final played?

23. The Soviet Union lost the first five international matches they ever played. How many goals did they score in total in these five matches?

24. Who was the first player to score a hat trick in a European Cup Final?

25. In the 1994 World Cup finals tournament in the US, which team scored the most goals in the first round yet failed to qualify for the latter rounds?

26. Even though it was their fifth appearance in a World Cup finals tournament, which team hadn't won a single game in a World Cup until the 1994 tournament?

27. How has Portuguese club Benfica honored their greatest ever player, Eusebio?

28. Which team won the Fair Play Award for the 1996 European Championship held in England?

29. For which national team is Heinz Hermann the most capped player?

30. Name the player whose last ever national team goal was the winner in a World Cup Final.

SOCCER PLAYER OF THE YEAR

Soccer Player of the Year (France Football Magazine)

1956 Stanley Matthews (Blackpool)
1957 Alfredo Di Stefano (Real Madrid)
1958 Raymond Kopa (Real Madrid)
1959 Alfredo Di Stefano (Real Madrid)
1960 Luis Suarez (Barcelona)
1961 Omar Sivori (Juventus)
1962 Josef Masopust (Dukla Prague)
1963 Lev Yashin (Moscow Dynamo)
1964 Denis Law (Manchester Utd.)
1965 Eusebio (Benfica)
1966 Bobby Charlton (Manchester Utd.)
1967 Florian Albert (Ferencvaros)
1968 George Best (Manchester Utd.)
1969 Gianni Rivera (AC Milan)
1970 Gerd Müller (Bayern Munich)
1971 Johan Cruyff (Ajax)
1972 Franz Beckenbauer (Bayern Munich)
1973 Johan Cruyff (Barcelona)
1974 Johan Cruyff (Barcelona)
1975 Oleg Blokhin (Dynamo Kiev)
1976 Franz Beckenbauer (Bayern Munich)
1977 Allan Simonsen (Borussia MG)
1978 Kevin Keegan (Hamburg)
1979 Kevin Keegan (Hamburg)
1980 Karl-Heinz Rummenigge (Bayern Munich)
1981 Karl-Heinz Rummenigge (Bayern Munich)
1982 Paolo Rossi (Juventus)
1983 Michel Platini (Juventus)
1984 Michel Platini (Juventus)
1985 Michel Platini (Juventus)
1986 Igor Belanov (Dynamo Kiev)
1987 Ruud Gullit (AC Milan)
1988 Marco Van Basten (AC Milan)
1989 Marco Van Basten (AC Milan)
1990 Lothar Matthäus (Internazionale)
1991 Jean-Pierre Papin (Marseilles)
1992 Marco Van Basten (AC Milan)
1993 Roberto Baggio (Juventus)
1994 Hristo Stoichkov (Barcelona)
1995 George Weah (AC Milan)
1996 Matthias Sammer (Borussia Dortmund)

FIFA World Soccer Player of the Year

1991 Lothar Matthäus (Germany)
1992 Marco Van Basten (Holland)
1993 Roberto Baggio (Italy)
1994 Romario (Brazil)
1995 George Weah (Liberia)
1996 Ronaldo (Brazil)

INTERNATIONAL WINNERS

Scores relate to Finals or play-offs. For tournaments played on a league basis, only the winning teams are listed.

World Cup
1930 Uruguay 4 Argentina 2
1934 Italy 2 Czechoslovakia 1
      (after overtime)
1938 Italy 4 Hungary 2
1950 Uruguay 2 Brazil 1
1954 West Germany 3 Hungary 2
1958 Brazil 5 Sweden 2
1962 Brazil 3 Czechoslovakia 1
1966 England 4 West Germany 2
      (after overtime)
1970 Brazil 4 Italy 1
1974 West Germany 2 Holland 1
1978 Argentina 3 Holland 1
      (after overtime)
1982 Italy 3 West Germany 1
1986 Argentina 3 West Germany 2
1990 West Germany 1 Argentina 0
1994 Brazil 0 Italy 0
      (Brazil won 3-2 on penalties)

Women's World Cup
1991 US 2 Norway 1
1995 Norway 2 Germany 0

European Championship
1960 Soviet Union 2 Yugoslavia 1
1964 Spain 2 Soviet Union 1
1968 Italy 1 Yugoslavia 1
      Replay: Italy 2 Yugoslavia 0
1972 West Germany 3 Soviet Union 0
1976 Czechoslovakia 2 West Germany 2
      (Czechoslovakia won 5-4 on penalties)
1980 West Germany 2 Belgium 1
1984 France 2 Spain 0
1988 Holland 2 Soviet Union 0
1992 Denmark 2 Germany 0
1996 Germany 1 Czech Republic 1 (Germany
      won 2-1 in sudden death overtime)

Copa America (originally called South American Championship)
1910 1st Argentina 2nd Uruguay
1916 1st Uruguay 2nd Argentina
1917 1st Uruguay 2nd Argentina
1919 Brazil 1 Uruguay 0
1920 1st Uruguay 2nd Argentina
1921 1st Argentina 2nd Brazil
1922 Brazil 3 Paraguay 1
1923 1st Uruguay 2nd Argentina
1924 1st Uruguay 2nd Argentina
1925 1st Argentina 2nd Brazil
1926 1st Uruguay 2nd Argentina
1927 1st Argentina 2nd Uruguay
1929 1st Argentina 2nd Paraguay
1935 1st Uruguay 2nd Argentina
1937 Argentina 2 Brazil 0
1939 1st Peru 2nd Uruguay
1941 1st Argentina 2nd Uruguay
1942 1st Uruguay 2nd Argentina
1945 1st Argentina 2nd Brazil
1946 1st Argentina 2nd Brazil
1947 1st Argentina 2nd Paraguay
1949 Brazil 7 Paraguay 0
1953 Paraguay 3 Brazil 2

1955 1st Argentina 2nd Chile
1956 1st Uruguay 2nd Chile
1957 1st Argentina 2nd Brazil
1959 1st Argentina 2nd Brazil
1963 1st Bolivia 2nd Paraguay
1967 1st Uruguay 2nd Argentina
1975 1st leg Colombia 1 Peru 0;
      2nd leg Peru 2 Colombia 0;
      play-off: Peru 1 Colombia 0
1979 1st leg Paraguay 3 Chile 0;
      2nd leg Chile 1 Paraguay 0;
      play-off: Paraguay 0 Chile 0
      (Paraguay won on goal difference)
1983 1st leg Uruguay 2 Brazil 0;
      2nd leg Brazil 1 Uruguay 1
1987 Uruguay 1 Chile 0
1989 1st Brazil 2nd Uruguay
1991 1st Argentina 2nd Brazil
1993 Argentina 2 Mexico 1
1995 Uruguay 1 Brazil 1
1997 Brazil 3 Bolivia 1

African Nations Cup
1957 Egypt 4 Ethiopia 0
1959 1st Egypt 2nd Sudan
1962 Ethiopia 4 Egypt 2
1963 Ghana 3 Sudan 0
1965 Ghana 3 Tunisia 2
1968 Congo Kinshasa (Zaire) 1 Ghana 0
1970 Sudan 1 Ghana 0
1972 Congo 3 Mali 2
1974 Zaire 2 Zambia 2
      Replay: Zaire 2 Zambia 0
1976 1st Morocco 2nd Guinea
1978 Ghana 2 Uganda 0
1980 Nigeria 3 Algeria 0
1982 Ghana 1 Libya 1
      (Ghana won 7-6 on penalties)
1984 Cameroon 3 Nigeria 0
1986 Egypt 0 Cameroon 0
      (Egypt won 5-4 on penalties)
1988 Cameroon 1 Nigeria 0
1990 Algeria 1 Nigeria 0
1992 Ivory Coast 0 Ghana 0
      (Ghana won 11-10 on penalties)
1994 Nigeria 2 Zambia 1
1996 South Africa 2 Tunisia 0

Asian Cup
1956 South Korea 2 Israel 1
1960 South Korea 3 Israel 0
1964 Israel 2 India 0
1968 Iran 3 Burma 1
1972 Iran 2 South Korea 1
1976 Iran 1 Kuwait 0
1980 Kuwait 3 South Korea 0
1984 Saudi Arabia 2 China 0
1988 Saudi Arabia 0 South Korea 0
      (Saudi Arabia won 4-3 on penalties)
1992 Japan 1 Saudi Arabia 0
1996 Saudi Arabia 0 United Arab Emirates 0
      (Saudi Arabia won 4-2 on penalties)

Central American Championship (CONCACAF)
1941 Costa Rica
1943 El Salvador
1946 Costa Rica
1948 Costa Rica
1951 Panama
1953 Costa Rica
1955 Costa Rica
1957 Haiti
1960 Costa Rica
1961 Costa Rica
1963 Costa Rica
1965 Mexico
1967 Guatemala
1969 Costa Rica
1971 Mexico
1973 Haiti
1977 Mexico
1981 Honduras
1985 Canada
1989 Costa Rica
1991 USA
1993 Mexico
1996 Mexico

Olympic Games
1908 England 2 Denmark 0
1912 England 4 Denmark 2
1920 Belgium 2 Czechoslovakia 0
1924 Uruguay 3 Switzerland 0
      Replay: Uruguay 2 Argentina 1
1928 Uruguay 1 Argentina 1
1936 Italy 2 Austria 1
1948 Sweden 3 Yugoslavia 1
1952 Hungary 2 Yugoslavia 0
1956 Soviet Union 1 Yugoslavia 0
1960 Yugoslavia 3 Denmark 1
1964 Hungary 2 Czechoslovakia 1
1968 Hungary 4 Bulgaria 1
1972 Poland 2 Hungary 1
1976 East Germany 3 Poland 1
1980 Czechoslovakia 1 East Germany 0
1984 France 2 Brazil 0
1988 Soviet Union 2 Brazil 1
1992 Spain 3 Poland 2
1996 Nigeria 3 Argentina 2
      Women's Tournament US 2 China 1

Asia Games
1951 India 1 Iran 0
1954 Taiwan 5 South Korea 2
1958 Taiwan 3 South Korea 2
1962 India 2 South Korea 1
1966 Burma 1 Iran 0
1970 Burma 0 South Korea 0
      (trophy shared)
1974 Iran 1 Israel 0
1978 North Korea 0 South Korea 0
      (trophy shared)
1982 Iraq 1 Kuwait 0
1986 South Korea 2 Saudi Arabia 0
1990 Iran 0 North Korea 0
      (Iran won 4-1 on penalties)
1994 Uzbekistan 4 China 2

THE MAIN LAWS OF THE GAME

Excerpts and summaries produced by DK from the 1997 Laws of the Game (approved by the International Football Association Board). Copyright © 1997 FIFA. All rights reserved by FIFA.

Law 1 The Field of Play (also see diagram below)
Flagposts
A flagpost is placed at each corner. Flagposts may also be placed at each end of the halfway line, outside the touch line.

Goals
Goals consist of two upright posts equidistant from the corner flagposts and joined at the top by a horizontal crossbar.
The goalposts and crossbars must be white.

Law 2 The Ball
The ball is spherical, made of leather or other suitable material, of a circumference between 27 and 28 in (68-70 cm), and weighs between 14 and 16 oz (410-450g) at the start of the match. The ball may not be changed during the match without the authority of the referee.

Law 3 The Number of Players
A match is played by two teams, each consisting of not more than 11 players, one of whom is the goalkeeper. A match may not start if either team consists of fewer than seven players.

Between three and five substitutions may be made depending on the competition. The names of the substitutes must be given to the referee prior to the start of the match. Substitutes not so named may not take part in the match. Any of the other players may change places

with the goalkeeper, provided that:
• the referee is informed before the change is made
• the change is made during a stoppage in the match.

A player who has been sent off before the kick-off may be replaced only by one of the named substitutes.

Law 4 The Players' Equipment
A player must not use equipment or wear anything that is dangerous to himself or another player (including any kind of jewelry).

The basic compulsory equipment of a player is: a jersey or shirt, shorts, stockings, shinguards, and footwear.
Shinguards are covered entirely by the stockings, are made of suitable material, and provide a reasonable degree of protection.

Each goalkeeper wears colors that distinguish him from the other players, the referee, and the assistant referees.

Any player who has been required to leave the field of play because of an infringement of this Law, and who enters the field of play without the referee's permission is cautioned and shown the yellow card.

Law 5 The Referee
Each match is controlled by a referee who has full authority to enforce the Laws of the Game in connection with the match to which he has been appointed.

The referee:
• enforces the Laws of the Game
• controls the match with the assistant referees
• ensures that the ball meets the requirements of Law 2

• ensures that the players' equipment meets the requirements of Law 4
• acts as timekeeper and keeps a record of the match
• stops, suspends, or terminates the match, at his discretion, for any infringements of the Laws
• stops, suspends, or terminates the match because of outside interference of any kind
• stops the match if a player is seriously injured and ensures that he is removed from the field
• allows play to continue until the ball is out of play if a player is only slightly injured
• punishes the more serious offense when a player commits more than one offense at a time
• takes disciplinary action against players guilty of offenses warranting a caution or being thrown out of the game.
• acts on the advice of assistant referees regarding incidents that he has not seen
• restarts the match after it has been stopped.
The decisions of the referee regarding facts connected with play are final.

Law 6 The Assistant Referees
Two assistant referees are appointed whose duties, subject to the decision of the referee are to indicate:
• when the ball is out of the field of play
• which side is entitled to a corner kick, goal kick, or throw-in
• when a player may be penalized for being offside
• when a substitution is requested
• when misconduct or any other incident has occurred out of the view of the referee.

Law 7 The Duration of the Match
Periods of Play
The match lasts two equal periods of 45 minutes. Any agreement to alter the periods of play must be made before the start of play.

Halftime break
Players are entitled to a break at halftime. The intermission must not exceed 15 minutes. The duration of the break may be altered only with the consent of the referee.

Allowance for time lost is made in either period for all time lost through:
• substitution
• assessment of injury
• removal of injured players
• wasting time
• any other cause.
The allowance for time lost is at the discretion of the referee.

Penalty Kick
Additional time is allowed for a penalty kick to be taken at the end of each half or at the end of periods of overtime.

Overtime
Competition rules may provide for two additional equal periods to be played.

Law 8 The Start and Restart of Play
A coin is tossed and the team that wins decides which goal it will attack in the first half. The other team takes the kick-off to start the match. The team that wins the toss takes the kick-off to start the second half. In the second half the teams change ends and attack the opposite goals.

Kick-Off
A kick-off is a way of starting or restarting play:
• at the start of the match
• after a goal has been scored
• at the start of the second half
• at the start of each period of overtime, where applicable.
A goal may be scored directly from the kick-off. After a team scores a goal, the kick-off is taken by the other team.

Dropped Ball
A dropped ball is a way of restarting the match after a temporary stoppage.
The referee drops the ball at the place where it was located.

Law 9 The Ball In and Out of Play
The ball is out of play when:
• it has wholly crossed the goal line or touch line whether on the ground or in the air
• play has been stopped by the referee.
The ball is in play at all other times, including when
• it rebounds from a goalpost, crossbar, or corner flagpost and remains in the field of play
• it rebounds from either the referee or assistant referee when they are on the field of play.

Law 10 The Method of Scoring
A goal is scored when the whole of the ball passes over the goal line, between the goal posts and under the crossbar.
The team scoring the greater number of goals during a match is the winner. If both teams score an equal number of goals, or if no goals are scored, the match is tied.

For matches ending in a tie, competition rules may state provisions involving overtime or other procedures to determine the winner.

Law 11 Offside
Offside Position
It is not an offense in itself to be in an offside position.
A player is in an offside position if:
• he is nearer to his opponents' goal line than both the ball and the second to last opponent.
A player is not in an offside position if:
• he is in his own half of the field of play
• he is level with the second to last opponent
• he is level with the last two opponents.

Offense
A player in an offside position is only penalized if, at the moment the ball touches or is played by one of his team, he is, in the opinion of the referee, involved in active play by:
• interfering with play
• interfering with an opponent
• gaining an advantage by being in that position.

No Offense
There is no offside offense if a player receives the ball directly from:
• a goal kick
• a throw-in
• a corner kick.
For any offside offense, the referee awards an indirect free kick to the opposing team to be taken from the place where the infringement occurred.

Law 12 Fouls and Misconduct
Fouls and misconduct are penalized as follows:

Direct Free Kick
Awarded to the opposing team if a player commits any of the following offenses:
• kicks or attempts to kick an opponent
• trips or attempts to trip an opponent
• jumps at an opponent
• charges an opponent
• strikes or attempts to strike an opponent
• pushes an opponent
• tackles an opponent making contact with the opponent before touching the ball
• holds an opponent
• spits at an opponent
• handles the ball deliberately (except goalkeeper).

Penalty Kick
A penalty kick is awarded if any of the above offenses are committed inside a player's own penalty area.

Indirect Free Kick
An indirect free kick is awarded to the opposing team if a player, in the opinion of the referee, commits any of the following offenses:
• plays in a dangerous manner
• impedes the progress of an opponent
• prevents the goalkeeper from releasing the ball from his hands.
An indirect free kick is also awarded to the opposing team if a goalkeeper, inside his own penalty area, commits any of the following offenses:
• takes more than four steps while controlling the ball with his hands, before releasing it from his possession
• touches the ball again with his hands after it has been released from his possession and has not touched any other player
• touches the ball with his hands after it has been deliberately kicked to him by a teammate
• wastes time.

Disciplinary Sanctions
A player is cautioned and shown the yellow card if he commits any of the following offences:
• is guilty of unsportsmanlike conduct
• shows dissent by word or action
• persistently infringes the Laws of the Game
• delays the restart of play
• fails to respect the required distance when play is restarted with a corner kick or free kick
• enters or re-enters the field of play without the referee's permission
• deliberately leaves the field of play without the referee's permission.

Offenses for which players may be thrown out
A player is thrown out and shown the red card if he commits any of the following offenses:
• is guilty of serious foul play
• is guilty of violent conduct
• spits at an opponent or any other person
• denies an opponent a goal or an obvious goal-scoring opportunity by deliberately handling the ball (this does not apply to a goalkeeper within his own penalty area)
• denies an obvious goal-scoring opportunity to an opponent moving toward the player's goal by an offense punishable by a free kick or a penalty kick
• uses offensive, insulting, or abusive language
• receives a second caution in the same match.

Law 13 Free Kicks
For both direct and indirect free kicks, the ball must be stationary when the kick is taken and the kicker does not touch the ball a second time until it has touched another player.

Law 14 The Penalty Kick
A penalty kick is awarded against a team that commits one of the ten offenses for which a direct free kick is awarded, inside its own penalty area and while the ball is in play.
A goal may be scored directly from a penalty kick.

Additional time is allowed for a penalty kick to be taken at the end of each half or at the end of periods of overtime.

Law 15 The Throw-In
A throw-in is a method of restarting play.
A goal cannot be scored directly from a throw-in.
A throw-in is awarded:
• when the whole of the ball passes over the touch line, either on the ground or in the air
• from the point where it crossed the touch line
• to the opponent of the player who last touched the ball.

Law 16 The Goal Kick
A goal kick is a method of restarting play.
A goal may be scored directly from a goal kick, but only against the opposing team.
A goal kick is awarded when the whole of the ball, having last touched a player of the attacking team, passes over the goal line, either on the ground or in the air, and a goal is not scored in accordance with Law 10.

Law 17 The Corner Kick
A corner kick is a method of restarting play.
A goal may be scored directly from a corner kick, but only against the opposing team.
A corner kick is awarded when the whole of the ball, having last touched a player of the defending team, passes over the goal line, either on the ground or in the air, and a goal is not scored in accordance with Law 10.

Kicks from the Penalty Mark
Taking kicks from the penalty mark is a method of determining the winning team where competition rules require there to be a winning team after the match has been tied.

Procedure
• the referee chooses the goal at which the kicks will be taken
• the referee tosses a coin and the team whose captain wins the toss takes the first kick
• the referee keeps a record of the kicks taken
• the teams each take five kicks
• the kicks are taken alternately by the teams
• if before both teams have taken five kicks, one has scored more goals than the other could score, even if it were to complete its five kicks, no more kicks are taken
• if after both teams have taken five kicks, both have scored the same number of goals, kicks continue until one team has scored a goal more than the other from the same number of kicks
• each kick is taken by a different player and all eligible players must take a kick before any player can take a second kick
• all players, except the player taking the kick and the two goalkeepers, must remain within the center circle.

Note: References to the male gender are for simplification, and apply to both males and females.

INDEX

ACKNOWLEDGMENTS

DK would like to thank:
Katherine Knight at the Football Association; adidas; Nike (UK); Reebok; Soccer Scene, 30-31 Great Marlborough Street, Carnaby Street, London; Umbro; UPC Sports Division.
Special thanks to Keith Cooper at FIFA.
Brihton Illustration Agency for soccer shirt and icon illustrations; John Plumer for wallchart map artwork; Nicola Studdart for soccer field illustrations on p.17, p.18, and p.90; Andy Crawford, John Garrett, Steve Gorton, Dave King, and Gary Ombler for photography; Richard Czapnik and Mike Buckley for jacket design; Steve Setford for additional editorial work; and Chris Bernstein for the index.

Special thanks to Jim Trecker for his review of text for accuracy, and for invaluable feedback regarding US Soccer vocabulary and philosophy.

The author would like to thank:
David Barber at the Football Association; Steve Greenall at Cambridge United Football Club; Richard Jones (Editor of Total Football Magazine); Keir Radnedge; Ray Spiller; Ray Wilkins; and all at DK.

DK would like to thank the following for their kind permission to reproduce photographs:
(a=above, b=below, c=center, l=left, r=right, t=top)

THE BOOK
Action Plus: 11cr, 12tr, c, Steve Bardens 26bl, Chris Barry 39bl, 60br, Tony Henshaw 44bl, Mike Hewitt 61br, Glyn Kirk 27cl, 28cl, 37tl, c, 47tc; **Allsport:** 26br, 29c, 30cl, bl, cr, 31tl, ca, 32cla, br, 41tl, 47br, cra, 55bl, 63c, br, 78cr, 81cra, Shaun Botterill 5tl, 19c, 35c, 55tc, 84cl, Simon Bruty 25bl, 37br, 43cb, 44bc, 82cr, 84br, David Cannon 2tl, clb, tr, 5tl, 25tr, 35cl, 40bl, 43br, 51crb, 55cl, 66bl, 82clb, 83tr, Chris Cole 25tl, Jonathan Daniel 84cb, Stu Forster 54tr, John Gichigi 23cb, Hulton Getty 36bl, 45tc, 46bl, 49br, 57cl, 62br, 64tr, bl, 71br, 76tr, bl, 77br, David Leah 20tl, tc, Clive Mason 54bl, Cor Mooy 39br, MSI 62tl, cr, 77cl, Craig Prentis 30tl, Gary M Prior 13br, 27ca, cr, br, 55tl, Ben Radford 14tc, 55br, 83tl, B Stickland 83cl, Mark Thompson 43bl, Claudio Villa 21c, 39tc; **Archiv Franta:** 71cla, t; **Archive Photos:** Reuters: Michael Urban 54br; **Associated Press:** 50c; **Bongarts Sportsfotographie:** 52tr; **Colorsport:** 5bl, 9clb, 11c, 13clb, cb, 15tr, 17cl, bc, 18clb, 22cb, 23cl, 24ca, 31tr, crb, 32tr, 35tc, 37tcr, cb, 38cl, 39bc, 41cra, cr, 42cla, 44-45c, 47cr, 50cr, bl, 59bc, cr, 60tl, 62c, 63tl, 64tl, br, 66br, 68cr, bc, 74clb, bc, 76crb, 79cr, clb, bl, br, 80tl, 80cr, 82tl, tr, bl, br, Stanley Chou 20br, 53br, bl, John Hawkes 24bl, Olympia: 5c, 21tc, 39tl, 57tl, Olympia/Galimberti 29cl, Tempsport/Liewig 23tl; **Comité Français d'Organisation de la Coupe du Monde de Football 1998:** 84tl, tr; **Confederation Africaine de Football:** 21cr; **Corbis-Bettmann/UPI:** 36cr, 76cra; **Editorial Atlantida, Buenos Aires:** 21br, cb, 72tl, tr, cr, 79cl, 80tr; **Empics:** Matthew Ashton 17tr, 18bl, 20cl, c, bc, 25tc, br, 31cla, 52bl, 55tr, cra, cb, Mike Egerton 31clb, Laurence Griffiths 11crr, 14cr, Tony Marshall 2cb, 22cl, 55cr, Don Morley 51clb, Steve Morton 28bl, br, 29br, 43c, 59br, Phil O'Brien 16tl, 40cr, Mike Poole 31bl, Presse Sports 50cla, cra, Sven Simon 57c, Neal Simpson 2tc, 5br, 29tl, 32cra, 45bl, c, 51br, 83cb, br, Aubrey Washington 30br, 53trb, Wilfried Witters 37cra, 58tl, 78br, 80br; **Europa Press:** 70crb; **Mary Evans Picture Library:** 4tc, 6, 7cr, 8cbr, clb, cl, bc, 9tr, 9b, 10tl, tr, c, 46cl; **The Football Archive:** 2b, cr, br, 3, 4tl, br, 19cl, 20bl, 20-21c, 21tr, 22-23, 23tr, 24cr, 25c, 27tl, 29tr, 35crb, 40-41b, 41c, br, 43cl, tc,

45crb, 48tlb, 51c, bl, 52bc, cl, br, cr, 53cl, bl, 56, 58cl, bl, 58-59c, 61tl, bl, 63bl, 67tl, cra, 70tl, 72cl, br, 73cb, 75tr, cra, crb, 77tr, ca, cra, bc, 78crb, tr, c, cr, 79tl, tr, 81tl, cla, b, 85; **Gremlin Interactive Limited:** 11bc; **Bryan Horsnell:** 4tr, 9tc, 10bl, br, 71crb, 73tr, 90bl; **Hulton Getty:** 4cra, 7tl, 8tl, 11tl, cl, brc, 17clb, bl, 18tl, cla, 28tr, 29bl, 34bl, 39cr, crb, 42bl, 45cr, 48cbr, crb, 49tl, 51tl, cb, 65tr, bl, br, 67bc, 68c, 70tr, cl, 71cra, bl, 73ca, bl, br, 74crb, 75cl, Allsport 65cl; **Kjøbenhavns Boldklub:** 9cr; **Mark Leech:** 31cla, br, 32tl, clb, bl, 84clb; **MTI Sport Dept:** 49tr, cr; **The Robert Opie Collection:** 8cr, 9cla, ca, cal, 10tcr, trc, 11cl, cb, 76tl, 90tl, tr, br; **Popperfoto:** 7b, 9tl, 19cr, 22tc, 22cr, 33, 34r, 35cra, cr, 38clb, bc, 39cra, 45br, 48cl, c, cra, cr, 49bl, bc, c, 49crb, 57cr, 60cr, 61cr, 63cl, 68tl, 69, 78tl, 80bl, Bob Thomas 35br, Tobias Rstlund 19bl; **Presse Sports:** 43cra, 51cra; **Rex Features:** 24tl; **Sporting Pictures:** 11br, 12cb, bl, 16tr, 18bc, 23ca, 37tc, cr, 38br, 43cr, crb, 47tl, cb, cr, 54tl, 58bc, 60bl, 62bl, 66cl, tr, 80clb, 81c, 82cla, 83cra, crb, 84bl; **Topham Picturepoint:** 1, 14cl, 26tl, 27bl, 35bl, 48bl, br, 50br, 67br, 70b, 73cl, 75bl, Associated Press: 74tl, cla, c, Press Association: 5tr, cr, 76cl; **Zefa Pictures:** K Goebel 4clb, 22c.

THE WALLCHART
Allsport: Shaun Botterill: Enrique; David Cannon: Ronaldo; **Colorsport:** Asprilla; Stanley Chou: Babayaro; **Colorsport/Tempsport:** Christian Liewig: Saint-Denis Stadium; **Comité Français d'Organisation de la Coupe du Monde de Football 1998:** France 1998 logo, Mascotte Officielle, Stadiums: Bordeaux, Lens, Lyon ©Berger-Ville de Lyon, Marseille, Montpellier, Nantes, Paris Parc des Princes, Saint-Etienne Ville de Saint-Etienne Christian Bruchet; Architects Berger/Jallou, Toulouse Ste. Absis; Architechts Ferret, Cardette and Huet, O.H.K-Setes.Seti; IGA-BET; **Empics:** Matthew Ashton: Sammer, Shearer; Tony Marshall: Batistuta; Neal Simpson: Bergkamp, Stoitchkov, Zidane, Zola; **Popperfoto:** World Cup trophy.

THE JACKET
Allsport: David Cannon back cl, Simon Bruty back crb, John Gichigi back bl; **Colorsport:** front bl; **Comité Français d'Organisation de la Coupe du Monde de Football 1998:** back cra, belly band; **Empics:** Matthew Ashton front tr; Sven Simon back br, Neal Simpson front br, back tr; **The Football Archive:** back tl, bc; **Popperfoto:** cr, belly band; **Sporting Pictures:** spine

Answers to national team questions
p.34 Mario Zagalo. p.35 Brazil defeated Bolivia 3-1. p.36 Hamburg in 1983 and Borussia Dortmund in 1997. p.37 Uli Stielike in 1982. p.38 North Korea. p.39 Bolt. p.40 Argentina 3 Uruguay 2. p.41 Argentina defeated the US 6-1. p.42 Bellone. p.43 Mexico. p.44 Van Basten. p.45 Feyenoord (beat Celtic 2-1 in 1970). p. 46 0-0. p. 47 Bryan Robson. p.48 Nasazzi. p.49 Austria p.50 Oleg Blokhin in 1975. p.51 Barcelona: 22 times, Real Madrid: 17 times. p.52 Denmark in 1985. p.53 Green Eagles.

Answers to Test Your Knowledge quiz, p.88
1. Ajax of Amsterdam. 2. Terry Venables. 3. The team was founded by an Englishman. 4. Jock Stein. 5. Newton Heath. 6. 50 years old. 7. 43 goals. 8. Bobby and Jack Charlton. 9. Bonifaci. Halftime. 10. Escape To Victory. 11. 1912. 9-0 (they defeated Finland). 12. The Hungarian Revolution. (He was in western Europe at the time and stayed on.) 13. Morocco. 14. The Vulture. 15. Grasshoppers of Zurich. 16. Jürgen Klinsmann. 17. 21 years of age. 18. 1933. Bulgaria. Spain defeated Bulgaria 13-0. 19. Stockport County and Leicester City (at Old Trafford). 20. The Gunners. 21. Penarol of Montevideo. 22. Paris in 1956. 23. 2 goals (they conceded 43). 24. Ferenc Puskas in the 1960 Final. 25. Russia. 26. Bulgaria. 27. By erecting a statue of him at the entrance to their stadium. 28. England. 29. Switzerland (117 caps). 30. Gerd Müller (for W. Germany, 1974).